"So, what do you think of Vella West so far?" Sloane's eyes were wide and vulnerable, as if she was asking about so much more than a resort.

"It's beautiful," Blake said. She had to admit that at least. This place had a way of sweeping you up into the romance of it all. "Doesn't it kind of remind you of..."

"It does," Sloane's lips curved, barely. "And thank you."

Blake looked at her. "So, this *is* your work then?"

"A lot of it is. I guess you could say I was inspired."

Blake could see Sloane's fingerprints—her perfect blend of old-world charm and modern elegance—all over this place. The restraint. The perfection. The way the space seemed designed to make you feel like the world was holding its breath just for you.

Blake leaned back, letting herself look—really look—at the woman across from her. Years had passed, but something in her felt young again. Still undone.

Sloane was here. Sitting across from her. At a table for two lit like a love story.

It was too much.

It was not enough.

Dear Reader,

I grew up in Northern California, where wildflowers bloom with abandon and the sunsets paint the hills in golden light. It's a place I know and love and I can't wait to share it with you.

When I sat down to write this second-chance romance, I imagined a setting as multifaceted and layered as Blake and Sloane's story. The wistfulness of young love revisited, both complicated and achingly real, demanded a setting that reflected the depth of their past and the promise of their future. Napa Valley, with its timeless charm and sweeping vineyards, was the perfect spot.

Blake and Sloane both doubt that they deserve happiness. Their paths back to each other are far from easy—marked by heartbreak, longing and the fragile promise of healing. Writing their story broke my heart in the best way.

So, welcome to Vella West, a luxurious winery and resort nestled in the heart of wine country, where the sweet scent of wildflowers mingles with the earthy vines lined in a row and the air hums with the promise of new love.

Jenny Lane

HOW TO RESIST YOUR BILLIONAIRE EX

JENNY LANE

ROMANCE

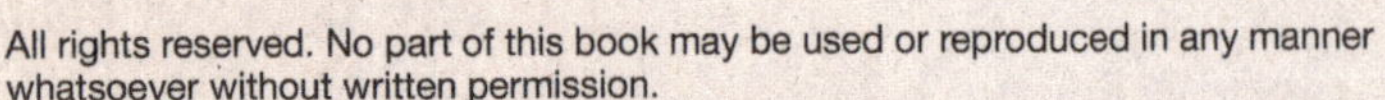

ISBN-13: 978-1-335-47077-5

How to Resist Your Billionaire Ex

For questions and comments about the quality of this book, please contact us at CustomerService@Harlequin.com.

Harlequin Enterprises ULC
22 Adelaide St. West, 41st Floor
Toronto, Ontario M5H 4E3, Canada
www.Harlequin.com

HarperCollins Publishers
Macken House, 39/40 Mayor Street Upper
Dublin 1, D01 C9W8, Ireland
www.HarperCollins.com

Printed in U.S.A.

Jenny Lane (she/they) writes contemporary stories with queer characters ranging from middle grade to adult. Their stories are queer, whimsical, heartwarming...and always end with a happily-ever-something. There is nothing Jenny loves more than a fire pit, an ocean view and a good book to read—but they will settle for any combination of these three. When she isn't writing or reading something, she works as a librarian and advocate for literacy.

Books by Jenny Lane

Harlequin Romance

Her Fake Wedding Date in Sicily

Visit the Author Profile page at Harlequin.com.

For Meaghan. And our three wildflowers.

CHAPTER ONE

Blake

BLAKE DIDN'T COME all this way to second-guess herself—not when something that looked a lot like a future was waiting just beyond those doors. So, she pushed the car door open before the driver had fully stopped, heart pounding like it already knew how this all would end. Her heel landed against the stone drive—a declaration, a step toward something she might finally be ready for.

She didn't let herself hesitate.

Her eyes followed a path lined with rosemary shadowed by cypress, before lifting to the entrance of Vella West. It looked like something out of a fairy tale: warm wood and stone features dropped in the middle of lush green vineyards and an endless sky. And Blake just knew that beyond those heavy oak doors, the story that was going to change her life was waiting for her.

Ivy trailed up the sun-warmed stone walls,

and antique doors that were no doubt imported loomed under an arch of flowering vines. She was sure their weathered wood contained secrets she couldn't wait to uncover. Bees hovered lazily over the bursts of indigo buds in the lavender planters and butterflies danced through the shafts of golden afternoon light.

Blake tightened her grip on her tote and continued toward the entrance. Her week here was meant to be work—an opportunity to prove she belonged at the writer's table—but something about this place made her feel like she'd already crossed a line. It was as if the social media manager version of herself that left San Diego that morning was already slipping away.

When Robby from PR at Vella West reached out to her on her magazine's official social media, she was certain it was spam. But she showed the message to Tara, her boss, anyway, and was shocked to find it was a real invitation. They wanted someone from her magazine to spend a week at their new resort next to the up-and-coming vineyard of the same name. It was a week full of surprise events and activities designed to wow the traveler.

The entire office got swept up in the magic of it. A flurry of whispered gossip and wild speculations. Vella West was the personal project of a young billionaire in the Napa Valley. It was said that half the resort was painstakingly imported from across the sea and the billionaire oversaw the placement of every stone. Blake couldn't help but get swept up in the magic herself. The whole thing sounded entirely romantic.

Everyone wanted a chance to visit the resort—including Blake. She'd known a head writer would get the assignment. But Ginny went and eloped one week before she was supposed to leave and cashed in her paid time off to spend her honeymoon cliff diving. Which left Blake the perfect opportunity to stop relying on what she was simply *good* at and start going after something she *wanted*.

"Let me go," she'd pleaded when she'd marched into her boss's office late that evening. "I can do it. I can leave in the morning."

"Blake, you know I love having you on this team. Your social media presence has transformed this magazine. But writing an article is different." Tara shifted in her leather swivel chair and frowned. "You don't even travel."

"That's not true," Blake countered. She wanted this. No. She *needed* this. This was her chance. "I've traveled before."

"When?"

"I backpacked through Europe before I started working for you." Blake didn't add that she hadn't *wanted* to travel since that glorious and heartbreaking trip ten years ago. Nothing would ever compare to it. And nothing could make her go through the same loss she felt after it. "I can do this."

She spread out her body, making herself big, as if she was facing a mountain lion and not her narrow-eyed, sharp-tongued boss who only came up to Blake's shoulders. She wasn't sure why her heart and her head had synced up over this assignment, but it called to her like a siren song.

"This exclusive review has already brought in tens of thousands of dollars in ads." Tara pressed her fingertips to her temples and spoke the next part softly. "If it doesn't hit, then we're not just looking at a loss for the quarter. I'm looking at a loss of the magazine."

"I have a degree in art history and creative writing. I can do this assignment justice. I *need* to see this place." She splayed her hands across her boss's desk and faked the courage she needed to say, "I can write a great article. And when I do, you'll promote me to travel writer. I've got this, Tara."

Tara sighed. "I'm probably going to regret this." She pushed a file toward Blake with the tip of her pen. "But if I don't send you, I'd have to go myself. And there's too much to do here." Tara glared at the looming stack of papers on her usually organized desk. “You can get the rest of the details from Chloe. And it better be good. Otherwise, not only will you not get a spot on the travel writing team, you might not have a spot at all.”

Blake knew this exclusive article was pulling in enough advertisements to meet their third quarter goal and then some. She knew exactly what was at stake. She and Chloe, Tara’s assistant, had speculated about it over lunch a few days ago.

“I understand.” Blake clutched the folder to her chest. She had wanted Tara to know she was going to take this seriously. Those words had settled like a stone deep in Blake’s stomach. She had been churning them around ever since.

But from the moment the town car pulled off the main highway and headed down the rambling country road, Blake couldn’t focus on anything except the feeling she was stepping into a memory. A hazy moment that felt like a sunworn photograph.

Memories of when she was fresh out of college, with nothing to her name but a passport and a backpack, spending days in the Italian sunshine, kiss drunk from the strawberry wine on Sloane’s lips. That had been an incredible summer. Just two women, girls really, whispering secrets and dreams as they lay on a blanket in a field next to an abandoned farmhouse, the trees providing latticed sunshine across their bare stomachs.

It had been love—not at first sight—but definitely fast and hard the way you can only fall when you're young and free and have nothing to lose. They were going to upend their entire lives for each other. Blake had quit her job via email—backing out of her internship-turned–assistant editor position at an up-and-coming magazine. She'd done it for the chance at adventure. At love. She could still remember how exhilarating it had been to watch the email whoosh away.

Sloane had seemed so certain about the future, about Blake. But one morning Blake had woken up and Sloane was gone—a scrawled note on the bedside saying she had to leave for a family emergency. Blake's panic and worry compelled her to leave voicemail after voicemail, until the inbox was full. She'd attempted to look Sloane up because maybe something awful had happened, but it was as if she'd disappeared without a trace.

Blake's worry turned to anger and then heartache. She turned it over in her like a jagged rock in a tumbler. It was still there, all these years later, a heavy and uncomfortable reminder of what happened when you let your guard down, even if the edges had smoothed out over the years.

Blake had never done anything so reckless, or so freeing, since. She'd returned from that summer in Italy and began an internship with a different, lesser-known magazine. If Tara hadn't rescued her, she'd still be fetching coffee on the seventeenth floor with no end in sight.

There was something about the yellow hills, the hint of dirt and earth in the air, that brought her back to the moment. Blake took in the main building—whitewashed walls with stone accents and tall windows, as if it was plucked from the hills of Italy. She'd read up on the place, sure, but seeing it in person was something else. Somewhere behind it, she knew, was the wine bar she planned to visit later.

Past the building, rows of vineyard stretched toward the hills, green and full in the early summer light. Her gaze followed the slope upward to where the cottages were tucked discreetly among the trees—private, just as advertised.

She caught the faint scent of lavender and turned. A stone path led to the spa and yoga studio, if she felt ambitious tomorrow morning. To the left, a string of bistro lights hung above long wooden tables in a garden space clearly designed for lingering evenings and curated dinners. All of it was exactly as she'd imagined—maybe better.

She was going to test out every inch of this resort and capture each moment for the write-up. The contract laid out exactly what she was expected to review. She could post sneak peek shots along the way for her magazine's social media if she wanted, and the full review would print after the week ended. So, this week was about soaking it all in. And Blake couldn't wait. She'd already made a spreadsheet of ideas and was looking forward to a meeting with Robby, the PR manager.

Two concierges opened the wide glass doors and smiled at her as she breezed through. The bright Napa sun warmed her back as she stepped into the lobby. The design of this place, with its slate gray–and-cream-checkered tiles lining the main lobby, was exactly like something from her travel Pinterest boards—the closest she'd come to actual travel in years.

She'd chosen a simple black dress for her arrival, hoping to impress the staff and encourage her own confidence. Her wavy brunette locks flowed down past her shoulders and her wide sunglasses hid most of her face. The black dress wrapped tightly around her waist before billowing out around her hips and falling just below her knees, flaring out in just the way she loved.

Blake did a wide slow turn, admiring the high ceilings, the wooden beams and the quiet trickle of a water feature she couldn't see. She took a slow breath to steady herself and scanned the room for the front desk.

From the side of the building, a door swung open and two people walked through. The first she recognized: Robby Berg, the PR manager she'd been in contact with. They had a short black shaggy haircut and the type of slim pants and button-down shirt that looked ordinary, but Blake was certain a designer insignia was stitched on the pocket. They kept glancing from their tablet to the woman they were talking to. The woman next to Robby had a sleek black bob, a sharp chin and an uncanny resemblance to—no—that was just Blake's memory playing a mean trick.

"Ah, Ms. Miller, you're here," Robby called from the other side of the room. They tucked the tablet under their arm and leaned close to whisper something to the woman next to them. Blake pasted on her most charming smile and turned toward Robby. "I want to introduce you to—"

The woman looked up and grinned broadly before freezing in shock.

Blake knew that face. She'd watched that face make promises it didn't intend to keep. Blake had been ready to follow Sloane across all of

Europe. In fact, they'd planned to do so. They were going to catch a train and go wherever the wind blew them for as long as it would last, seeking every dilapidated home until they found one to fix up.

But this woman, the one standing twenty feet away from her, was not, in fact, a figment of one of Blake's many dreams. She was here. In Napa. Walking toward her.

Sloane was real in a way Blake couldn't deny. She had the same sharp jawline Blake remembered, the kind that caught the light just right, warm olive skin and a sweep of dark hair that framed her face like a curtain falling perfectly into place. Her eyes—the deep midnight blue Blake had always gotten lost in—locked on her now, wide and unblinking.

Sloane's smile faltered as her eyes roamed over every inch of Blake. Like she wasn't sure what she was seeing. She looked like she'd seen a ghost. One she wasn't ready for.

Her mouth shaped Blake's name without quite saying it—more a whisper, a prayer, like speaking it aloud would cost her something.

Blake's throat went tight. There were a hundred versions of this moment she'd imagined. This wasn't any of them. It was better and a thousand times worse. Because she was mad at Sloane, still, after all this time. And the rock she'd thought she'd honed into a smooth and dull burden in her stomach launched into her throat, jagged edges tearing at her insides, making her feel sick to her stomach. Angry tears pricked at her eyes. She wanted to reach out and touch Sloane to prove she was real, but she balled her hands into fists, determined not to give Sloane the satisfaction of knowing exactly what she could still do to Blake after all this time.

Sloane, for her part, seemed completely unaffected—apparently living hours away this entire time with some kind of job in public relations. That was comical. Sloane, who couldn't pick up a phone, was in charge of relating to people.

Sloane took another step toward her and reached out her hand, but then must have thought better of it, because she immediately snatched it back. Sloane's eyes swept over Blake, taking her all in. Blake worked to hold still and keep the turmoil hidden beneath her surface.

A familiar wave of heartbreak washed over her, and instinctively, she shielded herself, her defenses springing into action. She couldn't trust Sloane. Even if her body ached to be wrapped up in a hug, her brain told her to stand her ground.

But nothing could have prepared her for the way Sloane's mouth dropped open, as if she'd seen a ghost—an unwelcome one at that—when she stammered, "What are you *doing* here?"

CHAPTER TWO

Sloane

SLOANE COULDN'T REMEMBER what she'd eaten for breakfast that morning, but she'd never forget the way Blake Miller looked as she turned and caught sight of Sloane in the lobby of Vella West. Shock and surprise and a flash of crimson creeping up her neck. Blake Miller looked stunning with her chestnut-brown hair down and loose and free. Sloane remembered how she'd knot it on top of her head when she was writing or hiking. And Sloane had loved watching her unspool it at the end of the day.

That was how Sloane always thought of Blake, which was to say more often than she should. When Sloane couldn't sleep, or when she couldn't make it through the last five minutes of a meeting, she'd imagine Blake with her hair falling loose like cinnamon swirls in the air. But it was nothing compared to seeing her now. Ten years older, frazzled from a day of travel.

Real.

Sloane wanted to pull her in for a hug and see if she still smelled like the floral bodywash she'd lugged around Europe like a prized possession. But that would definitely be weird. You don't get to throw your arms open wide for the woman you left in a youth hostel in Italy without saying goodbye.

"I'm here to write a review of this resort," Blake said as she threw her shoulders back. It took Sloane a moment to realize she was answering her question. Blake's nose scrunched when she was frustrated. It was scrunched now. "And I'm supposed to get checked in right now. It was—*nice*—to see you."

"Blake, wait." There were a million things Sloane wanted to say to Blake. But they all soaked into her tongue like dry wine. All she could do was stare. Blake obviously didn't want her apologies, not that she was sure how to apologize. Sloane had done what was necessary. To protect her family, to protect Blake from what Sloane was being asked to do.

She reached out one hand and placed it on Blake's arm. The connection felt warm, like sunshine on her shoulders when she was riding on the trail. "I hope you enjoy your stay. I'm certain Robby will take good care of you. It was good to see you."

Sloane didn't miss the moment that Blake's eyes flashed with heat. Blake was ready to fight—just like they had many times that summer. They were arguments that ended with both of them naked and tangled in bedsheets at three in the morning. It had always left Sloane's lips swollen from kissing and her body sore in the best way the entire next day.

But the heat cooled into something else entirely. A little wistful. Tired. Which was much, much worse. Sloane wanted to brew some tea, curl up on one of the hidden-away rooms of the resort and find out every single detail of Blake's life since they'd last seen each other.

But Sloane didn't do that. She didn't take down time to catch up with friends. She worked, she took care of Nico and she didn't think about what things were like before. There was too much to do to think about what might have been.

Still, she was dangerously close to offering just that when Robby interrupted. "Ms. Miller, welcome. As I said before, I'm Robby. It's so lovely to meet you." They shot Sloane a confused face of frustration before ushering Blake away.

And thank goodness. Sloane needed to get herself sorted before she could be around Blake. Robby took Blake by the elbow and guided her over to the check-in counter. Blake looked back over her shoulder once and Sloane offered her a head nod, too nervous to open her mouth.

Her phone vibrated in her pocket with a meeting reminder. Sloane took three deep breaths and walked toward the wine bar. She was late for a tasting with her head chef.

It didn't take her long to find Robby later that afternoon. Their office was on the fourth floor, directly opposite Sloane's. And they always left the door open to let in as much light as possible.

She leaned on the door and waited for Robby to look up. They didn't. She was about to clear her throat when Robby sighed.

"I know you're there. Your thoughts are *very* loud." Robby looked up from the stack of papers in front of them and raised a brow. "Want to tell me what that was all about?"

"You know I'm your boss, right?" Sloane pressed her lips together in an attempt to be serious. Robby rolled their eyes and went back to the computer screen clicking around until social media was up.

"Three thousand likes," Robby said as they pointed at a post with the doors to the resort. "Our followers are up and this one photo from her account has three thousand likes." They glanced at the computer and smirked. "Three thousand and seven. I don't know how you know her, but she is going to be good for the resort."

Sloane swallowed thickly and looked at the computer screen. "*Elsewhere?* Is that…this is her social media?" Sloane blinked at the screen. She couldn't see the other photos and thank goodness for that. When she'd left without saying goodbye ten years ago, she vowed she wouldn't look back. She did not know what Blake had been up to. She thought she'd be a writer. Not a social media influencer. But three thousand likes had to mean something. Her heart ached with sadness and pride.

"I trust you, Robby," Sloane said with a huff. "I was just surprised. Is this…she's the person you contracted to promote the hotel?"

"Sort of. She's with *Elsewhere Magazine*. She's going to write a classy review—and *then* post it all over socials. I *hope*." Robby crossed their arms over their chest and frowned. "I am very good at my job. I think her magazine's take on travel will really appeal to a wide audience. So, you need to fix whatever *that* was in the lobby. We need her, Sloane."

Sloane nodded. Sloane's plan for this resort hinged on bringing in a new generation to Napa. Showing them that a weekend at a winery wasn't all about wine. That you didn't need to be a sommelier to enjoy everything Napa offered. They'd crafted custom packages to ensure every experience was unique. And if they did it right, if they created enough buzz, then maybe they'd really make something of this resort.

And Robby was right. It needed to be perfect. Yes, she had her uncle's money, but she wasn't going to sink all of it into a resort that wasn't a solid investment. In four years, she would hand this all over to Nico. His care and legacy were entrusted to her, and this resort was a gamble. She needed this to work.

Sloane needed to smooth things over with Blake if she wanted any hope of a positive review. Any hope that Blake would actually enjoy herself. Hell, what if Blake was halfway home by now, all because Sloane had given her a weird look and then a head nod? She needed to fix this.

"She's still here, right?" Sloane asked, panic already clawing at her chest.

"Something tells me there's a story here." Robby leaned back in their chair and a chunk of black curls flopped onto their forehead. "Do I want to know? Do I *need* to know?"

"No," Sloane insisted. "Nothing you need to know. Just show me her file. What's planned for this week?"

Robby snapped back into work mode, leaning over Sloane and typing into the laptop. And it was right there on the screen: Miller, Blake. Elsewhere Magazine. How had she missed this?

This grand opening had to go off without a

hitch. She'd promised herself, and her cousin, Nico, that this was a sound investment. That her ideas were a sound investment.

And Sloane hadn't become a billionaire without a track record of sound investments. In less than ten years, she'd turned her uncle's mediocre vineyard into a thriving one. And then she'd bought the land next to it and together with Robby and Nico, they'd dreamed up the idea for Vella West Resort.

She really needed to call Nico. She had three missed texts from him this morning.

Work and her cousin had been her entire life for the last ten years. She drowned herself in work until there was nothing of *her* left in any of it. Until now. This resort had her pulse running through it. Every stone a piece of her heart.

Sloane had thrown herself into work to forget her heartbreak and grief. And it had worked. She replaced the emptiness Blake left in her heart with paperwork, planning and purpose. And now she was here—and the success of the resort depended on positive reviews and recommendations.

"And that's it. Just under a week. We conclude our contract with her Saturday night after the launch party. Then she goes home Sunday." Sloane looked up at Robby. They'd been chatting nonstop while Sloane was lost in thought. “You okay, boss?”

“It’s Sloane.” With a few key strokes she sent herself the pertinent details of *Miller, Blake*’s visit. She needed to do this herself. Nothing could go wrong. “I’ll talk to her, okay. I’ll apologize. I’ll…think of something.”

CHAPTER THREE

Blake

"THE HONEYMOON SUITE? Really?" Blake hissed at a wide-eyed Chloe on the other end of her FaceTime. A smile tugged at the corners of Chloe's mouth as she pressed her lips together, her eyes sparkling with suppressed amusement. "I had to sweep rose petals off my bed! Chloe, stop laughing."

Chloe's giggles subsided, replacing by a worrisome glint of amusement in her eyes. "Oh, come on. It can't be that bad."

Blake rubbed at her temples and frowned as she took in the oversized king bed, a bottle of red wine with two glasses and the 'congratulations on your marriage' card accompanying it.

"Chloe, there's a list of events in this folder." Blake waved the heavy folder with the itinerary at the phone and glared. "A list of *couples* events."

"Just bask in it," Chloe encouraged. "Who

doesn't love a bathtub on their back deck? That place looks gorgeous."

Chloe was right, of course. The added surprise of seeing Sloane had sent her stress level to a ten, a headache building behind her eyes. But Blake wasn't going to tell Chloe any of that. She narrowed her eyes at Chloe and pointed. "You did this on purpose!"

"Maybe I forgot to uncheck the couples' package? Maybe I thought you needed a little added luxury? Or, maybe it was all an honest mistake. I guess we'll never know." Chloe shrugged. "What I *do* know is you can't back out now. You're there. You have an article to write. And if you don't do it—then..."

She didn't finish her sentence. She didn't have to. If Blake didn't do this well, then the entire magazine was in trouble. *Elsewhere* needed her. Tara needed her. Chloe needed her.

"You're right," she sighed. "I hate when you're right."

"You love me. And you've got this. I'll make sure Tara knows you're right on track."

Chloe ended the FaceTime with a jab to the screen. Blake had to do this. She didn't have a choice. She was going to do these couple events. All by herself.

Blake did her best to forget about rose petals, and couples' hikes, and private cabana rentals by the pool. She especially tried to forget the fact that her first love—the woman who ghosted her ten years ago—was somewhere on this property. But memories of Sloane and their summer abroad played across her mind like a film montage of all her happiest moments—a highlight reel of something she'd never have again.

She'd tried to date, men and women, over the last ten years. But she never felt that inexplicable spark or connection with any of them. She'd never wanted to stay up all night just to keep hearing them talk. She'd never kissed someone for so long her lips grew swollen and tingly. And she'd never had someone look at her and see *all* of her. Not the way Sloane had been able to.

Blake groaned and rubbed at her eyes, trying to scrub away the memories. She grabbed the duvet from the bed and tugged until every last rose petal fell to the floor in a pile. She needed to put all thoughts of Sloane back into the box she'd shoved them into long ago. Blake let her frustration and anger settle over her like a shield. Sloane wasn't going to get to her.

Not this week.

By the time Blake had showered and dressed for dinner, she'd convinced herself that she would be just fine. She just needed to figure out her angle for the story, and then the romantic ambiance could morph into something else.

But the lingering look and the nod that seemed not so innocent when Blake had turned back around—that was familiar. Sloane would get that look before splashing her in the ocean or challenging her to a race along the sand. She'd get that look in her eyes before crawling into Blake's single bed in the middle of the night and wrapping their bodies so closely together Blake couldn't tell whose limbs were whose.

Okay, enough reminiscing. Blake had a job to do. She was going to represent her company well. She was going to have dinner in the five-star restaurant on the resort's premises. While the magazine would send a photographer out for the main shots, she wanted to include personal touches for sneak peeks on social media. She was doing two jobs this week, and she was going to do them both well.

"Ms. Miller, welcome to Niccolò's. We are so honored you could join us." A host with a crisp white shirt rolled up to his elbows and a long black apron practically bowed. So much for anonymity. "Please come with me. Your table is ready."

She followed him beyond the main restaurant and through an open set of wood and glass doors. The patio unfolded like a well-kept secret, alight in the warm glow of the early evening sun. The light slipped across smooth stone floors and glinted off glassware, turning every surface golden. Napa stretched out in the distance—vineyard rows brushed with light, the soft curve of hills disappearing into the haze.

Blake stepped out and paused. The space wasn't large, but it was exquisite—composed with a kind of precision that didn't announce itself—it just *was*. Tables were cut from travertine, raw oak or smoked stone, each paired with matching simple black chairs. The palette was warm and grounded—natural textures, soft lines, nothing overly designed. Just enough glass and brass to remind her this was money. Serious money.

She didn't need the full story to know the billionaire behind this had spent a fortune—not just throwing cash at it but investing in taste. Real, rare taste. The kind that didn't need to prove itself. Blake had been to her share of high-end restaurants, but this? This was restraint as luxury. Every detail felt curated down to the inch.

The glassware was impossibly thin. The ceramics had a hand-thrown look to them, each a bit irregular. Somewhere nearby, she caught the scent of grilled fruit, rosemary and citrus on charcoal.

She traced her fingers across the pale stone table, already cataloging questions in her mind. Robby would know who'd designed it, sourced it, styled it. And she *needed* to know. Whoever had created this space hadn't just built a restaurant—they made sitting down to a meal part of the experience.

Blake smiled to herself. She could get used to this.

"Ms. Miller, your table."

The host gestured to a small table in the corner of the patio—private, romantic and almost too perfect. A low centerpiece of freshly picked herbs and wildflowers looked as though it had just been gathered from the garden. Two place settings. Candlelight. Ambiance dialed to eleven.

Blake offered a polite smile. "Oh, it's just me. I'm dining alone."

The host blinked. "Oh? Is your partner not able to make it?"

She was going to kill Chloe. Beneath the host's perfect decorum, Blake still saw a flash of concern. She wanted to crawl underneath the perfect table scape to get away from the pity in his eyes.

"There was a mix-up with the reservations," she said quickly, her tone light. "It's just me this week. But it's beautiful—I love the flowers."

From across the courtyard, she caught a laugh. *Sloane.* Blake turned just in time to see her in conversation with a small group near the bar. She'd swapped her suit coat for something softer—a white button-down tank, almost sheer in the golden light. Black trousers, still tailored to perfection. When Sloane glanced over and their eyes met, Blake felt herself wilt a little in her seat.

God. Not like this.

The host had cleared the extra place setting with precision, stacking plates and utensils with just enough clatter to make Blake's cheeks burn. She sank back in her chair, resisting the urge to disappear under the tablecloth.

The couple seated nearby looked over with interest.

This was bad. Maybe she should just ask for the food to go.

"Blake, I'm so sorry I'm late." Sloane's voice drifted across the restaurant. The host froze, quietly glancing from the place setting to Sloane before placing each item back with precision. He must know Sloane. And whoever she was, she was important.

"What are you—" Blake's words were interrupted by Sloane's.

"Is it still okay if we dine together?" Sloane looked at her meaningfully. Like she was trying to rescue her from everyone's stares. But she was leaving it up to Blake if she wanted to be rescued.

And against her better judgment, she did.

Not by Sloane. In fact, Blake wished the person across from her was anyone but Sloane, with her effortlessly sleek hair, and her stupid long eyelashes and her frustrating way of making *everything* look easy.

"Sure," she said in a monotone. She gestured toward the chair across from her and raised a single brow. "Have a seat?"

Sloane nodded at the host and he finished setting the place. "I'm so sorry, Ms. Vella. I'll bring wine out right away."

Vella? Had he just called her Ms. Vella? But that would mean...no. This was Sloane Mitchell. Blake had seen her passport. Blake blinked, trying to hide the tsunami of emotions warring inside her. When did her name change? *Why* did her name change?

"Thank you, Vince. It's much appreciated." Sloane said the words soothingly. And the host, Vince, disappeared back into the restaurant.

Sloane stood across from her—quiet, almost careful. Like she wasn't sure she had the right, but had come anyway.

"I hope I'm not interrupting," she said, her voice low.

Blake looked up. Everything in her stilled as her eyes connected with Sloane's. Her heart was in her throat, which made no sense. Sloane didn't get to have this much say over her body. "It's fine," she managed to say.

Sloane hesitated, eyes flicking to the place settings. "Robby mentioned you booked the honeymoon package. Said you brought someone."

Blake shook her head. "I didn't. It was a mix-up with another writer." Sloane didn't need to know that this wasn't supposed to be Blake's story. And she certainly wasn't going to tell her that Chloe had purposefully booked up what was probably the resort's most extravagant package for just Blake.

"I wasn't sure," Sloane said softly. She didn't look away. "I wasn't sure if you'd want me here."

There was no judgment in her voice. No jealousy, no entitlement. Just something quieter—something Blake didn't have words for. Sloane didn't belong at this table.

A pause stretched between them—just long enough to feel it.

And it was as if that stretch of quiet held all ten years of silence within it. Blake's heart ached at the barely healed edges. How was Sloane able to sit down across from her so easily? She'd probably spent the last ten years coasting through life without a care in the world. Meanwhile, Blake had been barely keeping it together. She made sure her shield was locked in place.

Blake was not going to rile her up in the middle of a crowded restaurant.

"Just sit down already." Blake waved a hand at the other chair. The sooner Sloane sat down, the sooner they could get this dinner over with. Sloane could absolve herself of her guilt, and Blake could get back to work.

The silence settled again, looser now, but no less charged. Blake glanced down—the travertine tabletop, the hand-thrown ceramics, the delicate arrangement of herbs and blooms that looked like they'd been plucked from the garden seconds before sunset.

She was about to speak, when Vince returned, swiftly filling their glasses and disappearing again.

"So, what do you think of Vella West so far?" Sloane's eyes were wide and vulnerable, as if she was asking about so much more than a resort.

"It's beautiful," Blake said. She had to admit that at least. This place had a way of sweeping you up into the romance of it all. "Even the flowers feel handpicked just for me. Everything feels…chosen. Doesn't it kind of remind you of…"

"It does." Sloane's lips curved, barely. "And thank you."

Blake looked at her. "So, you *did* have something to do with all this?"

"A lot of it. I guess you could say I was inspired."

Blake could see Sloane's fingerprints—her perfect blend of old-world charm and modern elegance—all over this place. The restraint. The perfection. The way the space seemed designed to make you feel like the world was holding its breath just for you. It hurt to know that someone capable of such details could be so careless with Blake's heart.

Blake leaned back, letting herself look—really look—at the woman across from her. Years had passed, but something in her felt young again. Still undone.

Sloane was here. Sitting across from her. At a table for two lit like a love story.

It was too much.

It was not enough.

"How involved, exactly?" Her voice came out rough and low, scraping against her vocal cords. "I heard the server call you Vella. Is this all… yours? Are you married?"

Sloane didn't answer right away, but her gaze didn't waver. The smile that ghosted across her lips was soft. Sad. Like she wanted to tell her everything but couldn't. Or wouldn't. "No. Not married. My uncle had a vision for this place. I am just…helping to bring it to life. I took his last name to make it all—easier."

Blake's heart raced with a mixture of surprise and relief. She wasn't married—not that it would matter to Blake. Sloane could do whatever she wanted.

Sloane lifted the glass of crisp white wine to her lips and said just before taking a sip, "So, tell me about you."

"What do you want to know?"

"Everything."

"There isn't much to tell. After you, I mean, after that summer, I went back to New York. I interned for a terrible magazine. And then my boss, Tara, scooped me up. She quit and took me with her to a startup, *Elsewhere Magazine*. And the rest is…well, I'm here."

"So, you're a writer?" Sloane's eyes grew wide with something close to happiness.

Blake wasn't sure how to explain to Blake that she had taken a detour into social media nine years ago and never looked back. She'd embraced social media as if it was all she had left in the world, because at the time, it sort of had been. She was surprisingly good at content creation. Having something easy and dependable was nice. Blake was good at her job, and taking a risk hadn't paid off in the past. So, she was playing it safe. Until now.

"I'm a writer this week." She forced a laugh. "I'm ready to be dazzled by this place."

"Oh, this place will dazzle you, I promise." Sloane seemed to realize what she'd said because she sat her glass down and cleared her throat.

"What about you?" Blake asked. "What have you been up to? When did you start working your magic in hotels?"

Sloane laughed. Blake's cheeks flushed, but Sloane waved her away. "I'm not," she said quickly. "Not really. This is my first one."

"Well, you picked a good one to start at."

Sloane gave her a long look. Like she was trying to communicate something. But stopped. "I hope so," she breathed. "I spent years rebranding my uncle's vineyard. And now…now I get to do this."

Sloane had talked about her uncle a few times in Italy. He was a single dad with a struggling vineyard. Sloane wanted to help him. Apparently, she'd gotten her wish. "And what is it you want, Sloane?"

"I want to have dinner with an old friend. I want to drink good wine and stay in the sun too long. How am I doing?"

Friend. Old *friend.* The words were like a cool douse of water on Blake's speeding heart. What was she doing? Flirting with this woman after years and years. She was at work. This was business. Blake sat up straighter, mirroring Sloane's posture, and nodded once.

“Right,” she said. She lifted her glass and waited for Sloane’s to press against hers. “To old friends,” she said brightly. And when their glasses clinked, Blake shoved their past into her memories, where it belonged.

CHAPTER FOUR

Sloane

BLAKE LOOKED GOOD. Time had made her softer and rounder, but also harder somehow. The Blake she remembered was open and adventurous. The woman in front of her was guarded. Now she eyed Sloane with, not quite fear, but definitely suspicion. But her cheeks still pinked at the top when Sloane smiled at her and she still played with her necklace when she was talking.

She forced her eyes away and took another large gulp of her wine. She needed to stop staring at Blake.

"So, you live in Napa?" Blake asked.

It was such a simple question, with a million ways to answer it. And all of them seemed wrong. Sloane *did* live in Napa. She'd grown up here until her parents sent her to boarding school. And she'd returned here during college to work on her uncle's vineyard. And now... well now Napa was very much home. And also, sometimes it felt like the loneliest place in the world.

Her uncle was gone. He'd been gone for ten years now, a terrible car accident on a winding road not too far from the property. Sloane still hated driving at night. Her cousin, whom she'd made her whole world, was off in college. And her parents? Well, her parents barely spoke to her now. Which was fine by her.

Having Blake in front of her was overwhelming in a way Sloane didn't know how to handle. Just hearing her voice, seeing her face—it stirred something that Sloane had kept locked down for a long time. She wanted to let herself feel it, but the risk was too high. Sloane had survived these last ten years by keeping her heart safeguarded and locked away. Sloane had lost too many people already. She couldn't open up to Blake, not now when she was leaving at the end of the week.

People could hurt you even when they didn't mean to do it. Her uncle's death had been an accident, sudden and swift. But the hole he left behind never closed. Her parents had closed themselves off, with a selfish, cold retreat. And now her cousin—the one person she'd let herself love without fear—was gone too, chasing his future far from here.

So, she did what she always did. She pulled back from Blake.

"Yeah." She settled on a half-truth. "I have a place close by. The resort has been pretty demanding the last few months."

Sloane wasn't sure how much Blake knew—or how much she wanted to tell her. Sloane worked very hard to keep her identity under wraps because she didn't like the attention. She didn't want the press's pity. Her uncle's death still felt fresh and new, even ten years later.

But this was Blake, a woman who had seen all her most vulnerable parts. Could she share this, too?

"I can imagine." Blake gripped her cloth napkin tightly before smoothing it into her lap. She fixed her pointed stare on Sloane. "Too busy for phone calls even. Or messages."

Sloane winced. So, they were doing this. "Listen, I truly regret the way things ended. But I did what I had to do for my family." That was the understatement of the century.

She'd flown home from Italy like a zombie, and moved through a week of funeral preparations, then a week of settling into her new life. Sloane spent months barely hanging on, pouring what little effort and energy she had into Nico. Her cousin had only been twelve. Together they're learned how to pack a school lunch, survive all those first holidays alone. Together they learned how to laugh again, even through their grief.

By the time Sloane felt stitched together enough to reconnect with her friends, they were all gone. Off earning PhDs, running businesses or having babies. Sloane felt time slipping through her fingers. She'd wanted to call Blake. But so much time had passed and the missed calls from Blake had stopped. How was she supposed to call her with all her drama? Blake was the kind of person who wanted adventures and experiences and someone who could leave at the drop of a hat. Sloane was none of those things. Not anymore.

She couldn't say all that. So, she said, "I've been working hard these past ten years. And building a resort from nothing takes a lot of focus."

"Wait. This is yours? All of this is yours?" Blake blinked at her with wonder. She let out a low whistle. Sloane dug her fingernails into her palm to ground herself. It wasn't hers, not really.

"My uncle's," Sloane corrected. "But I'm in charge. Mostly. Unless you ask Robby." When her uncle passed away ten years ago, nothing felt like hers. She was a guardian, keeping the vineyard going in her uncle's name. Keeping it going for her cousin Nico. But this hotel was different. A tiny voice whispered to her heart that this place *did* belong to her.

"Oh. That's still really amazing." Blake took a sip of wine. And then another one. She watched Sloane with one brow raised over her glass. "So, this is what you've been up to all these years. Bringing a dream to life."

Sloane swallowed. Blake didn't know how close she was to the truth. How close Sloane *hoped* she was to the truth. Every time she chose a plate or a plant or a pedestal sink, she hoped her uncle would have been proud.

"Something like that," Sloane said with a crooked half smile. "This place is a dream come true. At least for me."

"Did you…did you know I worked for *Elsewhere*. Is that why…"

"No." Sloane practically shouted the word. Blake was a brilliant writer. She had no doubt the magazine selected Blake for her excellent work. And she didn't want Blake to think for one second she didn't belong here. "I promise. I had nothing to do with it. This was just a really, really wonderful coincidence. I do work closely with Robby. It's my job to make sure things run smoothly this week. So, I'll be around a lot."

There was that flush again. Sloane wanted to press her fingers against the hollow of Blake's throat and see if her skin was warm to the touch.

"I know Robby was expecting two people. I feel terrible having the honeymoon suite." Her voice wobbled a bit, and she let out an uncomfortable laugh.

"No, it's perfect. You should enjoy yourself. That's our best cottage. But, if I am remembering correctly, your itinerary is set up for two. I'll see what I can do to make arrangements—"

Sloane reached for her phone and began searching the schedule for the week. Everything was full. It was full of excursions, leaving no wiggle room. She'd promised Robby she would take care of this. And here Blake was, already set up for disappointment.

"I'll be fine," Blake said, a sharp edge of indignation coloring her tone. She sat up straighter and tucked a lock of hair behind her ear.

"You'll be fine…going on a romantic horseback ride for two tomorrow?" Sloane raised a brow. She wasn't sure why she was goading Blake. She *needed* Blake to do these events. She sent Robby a help! text message under the table. Their response came back swiftly and punched Sloane in the chest: You'll have to do them with her.

"Are you saying I can't handle it?" Blake threw right back. Sloane loved when she was feisty. Her eyes widened and her mouth pulled into a flat line. A faint flush spread across Blake's collarbones.

"No, that's not what I meant." Sloane's pulse quickened. For years Sloane had dreamed of seeing Blake again. She stared at the message, willing the words to change. There had to be another way. They'd only been together ten minutes and Blake was clearly annoyed with her. "Robby said everything is booked. But I—" she chose her words carefully "—would be happy to join you on the excursions."

Blake laughed, a short bark of disbelief, before catching herself. She seemed to consider something before speaking again. Sloane wasn't sure, but the slight tremor in Blake's voice and the way her shoulders slumped suggested that admitting she needed help was painful for her.

"Are you sure you can handle that?" Blake sat up straight and cleared her throat. "You have time in your schedule to show me around?"

Sloane saw the question for what it was: a test. Sloane had broken promises to her before. She couldn't do it again. If she was going to do this, she had to do it right.

"I will make time," she promised. "Friends?"

Blake tipped her head to the side and pulled her mouth into a tight smile. "Friends. And I expect you to be on time. Don't make me look foolish, Sloane." It made something churn in

Sloane's stomach. Blake really had moved on. She could sit across from Sloane at dinner, agree to hang out doing romantic activities, and be completely unfazed by it.

"Good." Sloane took a long gulp of wine, desperate for a pause in the conversation. She needed to get it together. Blake's slight smiles and somewhat bossy tone couldn't make her stomach flip. Not this week. "I forgot how pushy you can be when you want to get your way."

Blake blanched. "I am *not* pushy," she laughed. "You just don't know how to ask for what you want."

A memory of their last days together came back to Sloane. Blake pushing, not so subtly, to know what was next for Sloane. Sloane dodging the questions at every turn. She didn't want to ruin her gap year by talking about her unknown future. She wanted to lie in the sun and kiss Blake and not think about tomorrow.

But then Sloane had gotten that call. And all thoughts of running away with Blake had soberingly come to a halt.

Sloane hadn't had a serious girlfriend in the last ten years. Sure, there had been a few meaningless hookups, but nothing that lasted more than a few days and definitely no one she introduced to Nico. Sloane had convinced herself that it was the pressure of work, or her protectiveness over Nico; but maybe it was more. Maybe this hidden hope that Blake would return to her somehow was the reason she never let anyone else in. Sloane didn't have the courage back then to say what she truly wanted. And it seemed she still didn't have it now.

Their dinner devolved into painful small talk and Blake looking like she regretted telling Sloane to sit down. Sloane wished she could rewind the last twenty minutes and begin with honesty. That she missed Blake. She thought of her every day.

She wanted Blake to know she'd left in a panic upon learning of her uncle's death. That she was scared to call Blake and tell her everything, only to have Blake tell her she wasn't interested with Sloane if she had responsibilities. Blake had fallen in love with a fun, carefree version of Sloane. And she was anything but that now. Instead, she spoke vaguely about work and dismissed anyone who walked her way.

But Robby appeared at the edge of the dining room and gave Sloane a signal that said, *actually boss, it's kind of important—you better get over here right now.*

"I'm so sorry." Sloane rose from the table, she felt awful leaving Blake there alone. "There's something I need to check on." She could see the way Blake's shoulders slumped, even if she tried to hide it.

Robby's words echoed in her mind. Blake's article could make or break this resort. They *needed* a good write-up. And Sloane had promised Robby that she could handle Blake Miller. If that is what it took to ensure a great opening, she'd do it. A knot of anxiety tightened in her stomach; she was facing a week with the woman she'd abandoned a decade earlier, a woman whose frustrated glare promised a difficult stay.

"But, Blake." She waited until Blake looked her in the eyes. "I'll go with you tomorrow. I'll see you in the morning for the first event at the edge of the lavender trail."

CHAPTER FIVE

Blake

A SINKING SENSE of dread washed over Blake as she flipped through the color-coded, annotated itinerary inside her embossed folder the next morning. Blake was accustomed to doing things alone. She had no problem attending local events, trying out a new restaurant or hiking with a group of strangers in San Diego.

But these events were *designed* for couples. She was looking forward to the horseback riding and lounging in the cabanas by the pool. But some of the events were marked as surprises, only noting a time and a location. She really didn't want to be crammed together with Sloane, close-bodied, while they worked with clay or some other ridiculous activity.

Blake's stomach dipped; a nervous energy buzzed through her at the idea of Sloane leaning over her, arms covered in clay slip. She shook off the image and tried to focus on breakfast. But she could barely eat the fresh pastries and tea left on her doorstep. Even if the pastries looked delicious, with their golden-brown crusts and sweet aroma, with the handpicked wildflowers adding a touch of rustic charm to the tray.

The lavender path outside her door took her away from the main building and down a hill that led to a barn and stables. It was a rustic haven blooming before her out of the reedy yellow grass. A large wooden barn, a small cottage off to the side and a fenced meadow with two horses munching on grass.

The hills rolled up and around the grassy meadow, covered in precise rows of grapes growing on the vine. The creepers varied from young and thin to lush and overflowing. Blake knew nothing about wine making. But she loved the idea of seeing all these stages around her at once. A patchwork quilt of different hues of green—and a testament to patience and faith.

"How do you expect to ride in those shoes?" Sloane's voice felt rough as sandpaper on the back of Blake's neck. She hated that she knew what Sloane's morning voice sounded like.

"It's just a ride. These shoes will be fine." Blake turned to find Sloane brushing the hair of a gorgeous sable horse with a dark black mane. She glanced down at her tennis shoes and fitted jeans. "Will this not work?"

"Not for what I have planned." Sloane's brushing slowed and she flicked her heated gaze up Blake's body. "You still wear a size seven?"

Blake cleared her throat, pushing aside the odd sense of comfort that even though Sloane hadn't remembered to call—or write—in the last ten years, she somehow still remembered Blake's shoe size.

"Yeah."

Sloane tipped her head toward the barn and walked away, leaving the horse staring curiously at Blake. Blake didn't want to give Sloane the satisfaction of trailing after her, but she *did* want a pair of boots.

Sloane passed the stables and headed to the small building. There was a tiny black placard in the grass just next to the door. *Private Property. Please do not enter.* Apparently, rules didn't apply to Sloane, because she flipped up the latch and slipped inside the small house. Storage room? Cottage?

"Are you sure I'm allowed in here…" Blake's words trailed away as she stepped into the cozy space. There was riding equipment, yes, but there was also a small love seat. A desk. A soft mint-green wall with a brass bed pushed against it. Blake felt as if she had stepped into a dollhouse. A dollhouse with very expensive furnishings and a saddle.

“What is this place?” Blake asked.

“Just a cottage,” Sloane replied, her tone suggesting the question didn’t need further discussion. She opened a small cupboard and plucked a pair of well-worn but immaculate boots. She thrust them toward Blake. “There. Now you can ride.”

Blake blinked at her. “Is this…yours?”

Sloane wiggled the boots, waiting for Blake to take them. “Yes? This is where I sleep usually. You can put them on over there.” Her eyes flicked to the loveseat; a bright green thing that looked like shoots of summer grass sprung up inside this tiny house.

“Why do you have a tiny house here when there is an entire resort a five-minute walk away?”

“This just feels like home.” Sloane looked around the space as if seeing it for the first time. Blake looked, too. Everything was simple, understated and soft. Luxury hidden beneath homey antiques, high-pile rugs and a homemade quilt.

Sloane winked at Blake and leaned against the wooden beam separating a kitchenette from the living room. “I can’t tell you all my secrets, Miller.”

“I don’t think I know *any* of your secrets,” Blake huffed. She dropped onto the couch and put on the boots, just so she'd have something to do. "I didn't even know you liked horses," she mumbled.

Sloane hmm'd to herself. "I don't. I like *one* horse. And she's going to be very mad if we don't get going soon."

"Where is everyone else?" Blake reached for her phone to triple-check the itinerary.

"The rest of the group already left. They're taking the easy trail around the pond." Sloane pressed her lips together as if trying to stifle a smile. "But I had something else in mind. Will you let me show you some of my favorite parts of this place?"

Blake bit back her frustration. Sloane loved to do this, surprises, adventures, unexpected little somethings.

Sloane must have seen the look on her face because she paused, tucked her hair behind her ear and said, softer, "Think of it as a behind-the-scenes tour. Still completely reviewable."

Blake exhaled deeply. "Fine." Once outside, she approached the gentle horse slowly, thoughtfully, and scratched at her muzzle. "I suppose a sneak peek and exclusive tour is kind of cool. But I get to ask some interview questions. Deal?"

"Deal."

"Good. Lead the way, Sloane."

Sloane

They'd only been on the trail for a few minutes when the questions started.

"So, how long have you been in California?"

How did Sloane explain this? That she'd always been in California. That these hills were her backyard. And also that she hadn't really existed at all since she'd returned from Europe ten years ago.

"Practically my whole life. I went to college in New York, but otherwise I've been here."

That was an easy one, but Sloane didn't love the idea of Blake digging around in her past. The next few questions were also simple. Favorite kind of wine, best markets in the area, spa treatment recommendations. But then the real questions started and Sloane began to sweat.

"And when did you start working for your uncle?" Blake fired off questions like they were in a courtroom. Not unfriendly, but not familiar. Was she hiding a recording device somewhere? Blake's brow furrowed slightly as she waited for answers. Well, she was going to have to wait a bit longer.

"Sorry, not today, Miller. I want to talk about you now." Sloane looked back to see Blake absently threading her fingers between Winnie's hair, trying to hide her annoyance. "How long have you been writing for your magazine?"

"About a week," Blake said. There was something tense in her voice that made Sloane want to know more. Want to know everything.

"A week? How did you manage this assignment after a week?"

Blake's cheeks flushed. Or maybe it was from the morning sun. Sloane should have given her a hat. Or smoothed some sunscreen across her cheeks and down the back of her neck. Nope. She definitely shouldn't have done that.

"I've worked for the magazine longer than a week. I'm the social media manager. I post teasers and links to articles. That sort of thing." She paused for a moment, seeming to weigh whether she could trust Sloane. Sloane bit down on the inside of her lip, and tried not to give away how interested she was in knowing more. "But this is my…my chance to be a *writer*. I came here for a story. And I have to admit, this horseback riding experience certainly is good. Do all guests have access to the stables?"

Sloane turned back around and waited a few beats before responding. "No," she said finally. "I have a friend who brings their horses to us when we organize an experience. But Winnie and Rhett…they're mine."

Sloane had wanted Blake off the resort's property somewhere private, away from Robby's interruptions. She didn't think she could handle being part of a guided tour of her own hills, with resort guests asking questions.

She wanted to bring this new *walls-up* version of Blake somewhere safe. Somewhere she didn't have to be *Sloane Vella*, owner of Vella West. But out here, on the trail, with the vineyards rising around them like sentient chaperones—watchful, silent and unbearably aware—she realized how impossible that was.

This was her sanctuary, the one place she let herself breathe. Sloane had spent years hiking these hills, learning herself as well as the landscape. She was quieter now. Letting her actions and her management of the property speak for itself. She had hardened herself against the years of solitude.

Now Blake was in it, and the air felt thinner. The vines seemed to close in, not just watching, but reminding her exactly how much she stood to lose. Maybe Blake wasn't the only one with walls up.

"You know, if you want me to give this place a good review, you're probably going to want me to see some of the amenities that are actually available." Blake raised a brow. Sloane huffed out a breath that wasn't quite a laugh and shrugged.

Blake was right. She was here for a job, for a shot at something real. *A chance*, she'd said. And Sloane knew that's what she had to give her. She couldn't offer an apology, couldn't explain why she'd disappeared ten years ago without a word. But this—this opportunity—she *could* give her that much.

"Well, in that case, maybe we'd better head back." Sloane tugged gently on the reins, and her horse responded, though he turned his head as if questioning her decision. "I'm sure we can arrange a spa day. Or a wine tasting."

"Are you kidding?" Blake nudged Winnie forward until they were even again. She looked good in Sloane's boots. Good on her horse. She looked good in everything.

"You promised me an adventure, Sloane. I intend to hold you to it."

With a click of her tongue, Blake urged her horse ahead, slipping into the lead. Not quite a gallop—but fast enough that Sloane would have to move if she wanted to keep up.

Blake could ride. She could *ride*. This woman was going to be the death of her.

Sloane closed her eyes and bit back a curse. "Come on, Rhett," she murmured into the horse's ear. "Let's go get your girl."

Rhett had been on loan from a friend the summer Nico stayed with her after his freshman year of college. But by the end of that week, Rhett had made up his mind: he belonged to Winnie. He'd followed her across pastures, refused to eat unless she was nearby, once even cleared a fence just to stand beside her. It was ridiculous—how certain he was. How stubborn.

When it came time to send him back, she couldn't do it. It had cost her. But it had been worth it.

The horse seemed to side-eye her with quiet judgment. He was known to throw riders out of their saddle and Sloane usually left him alone. But he must have taken pity on her because he shook his head and took off in Blake's direction.

Blake was riding Sloane's horse, a gentle, but fabulous caramel-colored mare. And she looked damn good doing it, too. They chased each other through the hills. Sometimes Sloane would pull into the lead and other times she enjoyed trailing behind Blake. Sloane thrilled at having Blake here, laughing and asking questions, and pulling her hair up off her neck when she needed to cool down.

They wound up by a small pond at the farthest edge of Sloane's property, well past the resort's boundaries. The sun glinted off the water, painting the meadow in a late morning glow. Sloane hopped off her horse and walked over to Blake.

"It's going to be hot today, isn't it?" Blake

asked. Sloane didn't respond. She walked closer and held out her arms. "What? You're going to help me down?"

"Obviously."

Blake scoffed as she adjusted the reins and prepared to dismount. "Sloane, I know how to get down from a horse."

"Humor me." Blake's stubbornness hadn't changed, at least. Sloane held up a hand and offered Blake one of her half smiles. "Winnie can be fickle."

Blake sighed but nodded. "Fine."

Sloane regretted the offer as soon as Blake's body pressed against hers. Blake slid down quickly, her body falling into Sloane's as she steadied her, digging her fingers into the soft flesh of her waist. Blake was warm and solid and smelled like every good memory Sloane had ever had. She'd wanted to bottle that summer up and bring it home with her.

"You can let go of me now." Blake's voice was a whisper in the hollow of Sloane's throat. This was the first time they'd touched in over ten years. Sloane forgot how Blake's mouth was right at neck level, in the soft skin of her throat. It used to drive her wild. It used to drive Blake wild, too. She'd told Sloane as much whenever she kissed the spot just below her jaw. She'd said she loved the direct access to the part of Sloane's body that turned her into a puddle.

"Right," Sloane said. She cleared her throat and stepped back. Space. She needed space. And maybe some water. Her throat was parched. Blake's probably was, too. "Here, have some water." Sloane reached into her bag and pulled out a canteen.

"Well, you're prepared." Blake smiled. "Thanks. Far cry from when we would head out for an adventure with nothing but our swimsuits and a few euros in our back pockets."

"It did lead to some great discoveries though." She took a drink from the canteen, realizing too late that Blake's mouth had just been in the same spot. The cool water did nothing to stop the blaze of heat in her belly.

"What else do you have going on today? I'm sure you're incredibly busy." Blake's words hit Sloane with a jolt. A quick glance at her watch reminded her she was ten minutes late for a meeting with a local vendor. She was going to lose the contract if she didn't get there soon.

"Yeah, we should get back." Sloane thought of Blake eating dinner alone tonight. The way she'd ignore everyone else in the dining room as she sipped her wine. She couldn't bear to think of it.

"There is a dinner tonight for some of the local vendors. Would you like to come?"

“That isn’t on my itinerary. I’m supposed to go to the pool and then to a—”

“I would really love it if you’d come. It’s not a big event. Just some local friends. It’s strictly off the journalism circuit.”

“I don’t think that’s such a good idea.” Blake went quiet. “We can let the past be in the past, Sloane. You don’t have to host me this weekend. I’ll be fine. I know you said you would do some of the events with me. But we don’t have to eat every meal together.”

“No,” Sloane said. “I want you there. I know I don’t have any right to say this, but I want to see you again. I want to know more about what you’ve been up to.”

“Sloane. You had ten years to do that.”

“I know. I—” Her words cut off and she looked away. She wasn’t going to get into this with Blake. Not when this morning had been sort of lovely, despite Blake’s initial coldness and her own awkwardness. “I can’t change the past, but I’d like to move forward. I told you I would do the events with you and I meant it. I want to keep this promise, if you’ll let me.”

Blake studied Sloane for a long time. Long enough that she felt her eyes everywhere. Then Blake shrugged. “Fine. What do I need to wear tonight? If it’s another boots situation I’d like to be prepared.”

Sloane bit down on her lip to keep from smiling. Blake looked good in her boots. Blake looked good in everything though. It occurred to Sloane that maybe Blake wasn't ready for an evening with the who's who of Napa Valley. Blake liked to be in charge, she wanted to know what was happening in every situation.

Sloane didn't want to overwhelm her, but she could at least ease this one burden. "Don't worry about that part," Sloane said. "I've got you covered."

CHAPTER SIX

Blake

BLAKE WANDERED TOWARD the pool, hoping that the warm air and sunshine would ease the restless thoughts swirling in her mind. She needed space—some distance from the weight of her emotions, the frenzy of her day, the quiet ache in her chest that wouldn't let her go. Blake knew this week would change her, but she certainly hadn't expected it to transport her back ten years.

The pool area was a work of modern elegance—a stark contrast to the vineyard's rustic charm. This wasn't just any resort pool; it felt like an exclusive oasis, the kind of place designed to make you forget that time existed outside its walls. Water shimmered in hues of aquamarine, the sun reflecting off it like a million tiny diamonds. Warm, golden light spilled across the space, kissing the edges of Blake's shoulders as she surveyed her options.

Tall cypress trees edged the perimeter, creating a barrier between Blake and the outside world. A few sleek white cabanas lined one side of the pool, each one a tiny sanctuary with thick, plush towels draped over loungers and small tables topped with chilled water and delicate sprigs of rosemary. The space was curated for tranquility—isolated yet welcoming.

Blake moved slowly, her feet cool against the stone as she walked, the soft scent of jasmine and fresh grass filling the air. Blake looked around the peaceful, open space. She wanted the quietest corner, the one that might hold her thoughts without judgment. The lounger she chose was near the far end of the pool, just a few steps away from where the water lapped gently at the stone. Kicking off her sandals, she let the weight of her day dissipate.

She draped the plush towel over the lounger, the fabric soft beneath her fingertips. Blake slid onto the chair, stretching out and tilting her head back, letting the sun bathe her in warmth. She closed her eyes, finding comfort in the murmur of voices, the breeze, and the water's gentle rhythm. For a few moments, she could exist in the quiet, letting the world spin on without her.

"Miss Miller?" A voice forced her to open her eyes and sit upright in her lounger. An unfamiliar staff member with a neat silver name tag and a crisp white polo shirt looked at her expectantly.

"Yes?" She shaded her eyes and looked up at the woman. She was young and held on to a crisp white envelope as if her job depended on it.

"This is for you," she said. "I'm so sorry to interrupt you. Is there anything else I can get for you?"

"Thank you so much. I'm good here." Blake took the envelope and the woman left. The expensive paper weighed heavily in her hands. If she hadn't seen her name printed across the front in Sloane's neat handwriting, she would have thought the woman had made a mistake.

The ink was blurry and imperfect where Sloane's pen had brushed the paper, as though she hadn't been entirely sure how to say what she was feeling. Blake hesitated at first, her fingers hovering over the edges of the letter. *Was she ready for this?* But she couldn't help it. She traced the words with her fingers as if the paper held something deeper—something unsaid, something both terrifying and thrilling.

The note, with its clumsy words, felt so... vulnerable. Sloane had written it by hand, and somehow, that small act of putting pen to paper made it feel more personal than anything typed on a screen could ever be. Blake lingered over the words as though they were a puzzle she couldn't quite solve, but wanted to.

Blake,
I had a really nice time riding with you this morning. If you're still up for dinner tonight, I took the liberty of sending you a dress. It's waiting in your room. I'll meet you at seven in the lobby, if you're still open to it.
Sloane

If you're still open to it.

That part kept echoing in Blake's mind. Sloane hadn't just written a note; she'd put her own hesitance on paper. Just when Blake had enough distance from Sloane to get some perspective, Sloane had to do something like this. A note. A handwritten note. She had to know what this would do to Blake. Sloane was playing dirty, and Blake couldn't help but smile at the thick paper in her hands.

And then there was the dress. If Sloane thought she could throw expensive clothing or lavish gifts at Blake and expect all to be forgiven, she was sorely mistaken. Blake's forgiveness didn't have a price tag on it. And she'd tell Sloane as much the next time she saw her.

She squeezed her eyes shut and let out a groan of frustration before glancing at the pool again, the water still and inviting. Maybe she could just let go of it all. Her anger and frustration at

Sloane. Her worry about work. She could dive into the clear weightlessness of the pool and just…give in.

But the thought of that note—it's quiet promise and uncertainty—refused to let her go. It wasn't just a letter; Sloane had *written* to her. Sloane, who remembered she liked little notes and gestures, had taken the time to write to her. It was misguided at best, but at least it was a start.

She wasn't ready for tonight. But maybe she never would be.

Sloane

Sloane paced the lobby of Vella West, her eyes flicking to the door every few seconds. It was nearly time for dinner, and Blake was still nowhere to be seen. A familiar knot tightened in her stomach. Maybe the note had been a mistake. She'd picked up her phone to text Blake and realized that she didn't know her number. And before she could help herself, she was grabbing her favorite stationery and taking a risk.

But now she wasn't here, and Sloane was going to be late and she'd bought that dress. Sloane was just trying to make things easier… but she was pretty sure she'd gone and messed up any chance of redemption with Blake.

She had told herself she wasn't nervous, but that wasn't true. She was pacing, her breath a little quicker, her pulse a little too loud in her ears. *It's just dinner*, she reminded herself. *Just dinner.* But if she was honest, she knew tonight was about more than just food and wine—it was the first real opportunity to see if all the years between them had truly erased everything. To see if Blake still wanted to know her, when she knew everything about her.

When she had picked out the dress for Blake, she'd told herself it was nothing, just a small gesture. A way to ensure that Blake felt at home with the crowd tonight. But even as she thought that, her stomach twisted. What if Blake didn't want to be reminded of what they had been? What if all of this was *too much*?

Just as she was about to pace toward the dining area, the doors to the lobby swung open, and Blake walked in.

Sloane's breath caught in her throat.

Blake was standing there, looking like the ocean at high tide. The dress looked soft as silk under the lighting, the simple linen clinging to the rounded curves of her body, the hem just brushing the tops of her sandals. She looked stunning.

She looked perfect.

She looked smug—because this wasn't the dress Sloane had selected for her.

This dress wasn't extravagant, but it was perfect. Blake left her hair down; the soft curls framed her face in loose waves, her cheeks flushed from an afternoon by the pool. She looked *effortless*—stunning in that relaxed Northern California way that made Sloane's pulse race.

For a second, everything stood still. Blake wasn't the naive, young girl she'd been in Europe. She was confident, glowing and walking right toward Sloane.

Sloane shook herself from her stupor, her heart hammering in her chest. She quickly composed herself and walked over, her voice steadier than she felt. "There you are," she said, her smile pulling at the corners of her mouth. "You look… stunning."

Blake's eyebrow arched, and a teasing smile tugged at her lips. "Thank you."

Sloane laughed, the sound coming easier than she expected. "You didn't like the one I sent?"

Blake's smile softened, and for a brief moment they just stood there, gazing at each other. The years between them, the silence, the uncertainty—it all seemed to fade in that look. For a heartbeat, it was like nothing had changed.

"I don't know—I didn't open the garment

bag." Blake's shoulders moved up in a soft shrug. It made her cinnamon swirl curls dance. "You can't buy me, Sloane. If you want to impress me, money isn't the way to do it."

A flush of heat crawled up the back of Sloane's neck, shame tagging along with it. That wasn't what she'd been doing...was it? She just wanted Blake to feel confident walking into tonight's dinner. That's all. So, she'd—okay, yes, she'd spent a ridiculous amount of money on a dress to prove she cared. Damn it.

"Well, probably for the best," she said, breaking the silence. Sloane swallowed back her pride. Blake's words were harsh, but not angry. This was progress. "This dress is a much better choice. I hope you're hungry," Sloane said, her voice low. She took a step forward, leading Blake toward the private dining room.

As they walked through the main lobby and then down another hall, Sloane could feel Blake at her side. Quiet but firm. The pull between them hadn't gone anywhere—it was still there, stronger than ever, and it made Sloane ache.

The vineyard's private tasting room was Sloane's third favorite place on the property, next to her cottage and the wildflower fields. It had a retractable wall of glass windows connected to the patio off the south side, with views of her stables and pond in the distance. Dining here felt intimate and wide-open all at the same time.

The table was grand, set with gleaming custom drink ware and sophisticated silverware, each course meticulously presented. The air was fragrant with the aromas of fine wine, fresh herbs and expertly prepared dishes. The panoramic view of the Napa Valley vineyards past her own property stretched beyond the open doors, bathed in the warm glow of the setting sun.

Sloane couldn't help but look at all of it with new eyes. What must Blake think of all this? The Blake from ten years ago probably would have been unconvinced. But, then again, Sloane would have been overwhelmed, too. She took a deep breath and reminded herself that they'd both changed a lot in the last ten years. And she wanted to see what Blake had become.

As the night unfolded, the conversation at the table swirled around them—business deals, the latest vineyards and casual talk of family and life in Napa's bubble. It was all a bit too polished, too perfect for Sloane, who was always more at home in the vineyards, riding her horse or with her sleeves rolled up. But she could turn on the charm when she had to.

"Sloane, how's Nico? Why isn't he here?" Glenn was her uncle's best friend and friendly vineyard rival. When Sloane had taken over, he'd shown her the ropes and looked out for her and Nico. "I didn't think he'd miss a week like this."

He meant his question kindly, but it made Sloane tense. Her eyes darted to Blake, who pretended not to listen, but there was a hunch in her shoulders. She needed to tell her about her cousin. Blake deserved to know everything. But in the middle of a large dinner party was not the place to explain.

"He's still in school," Sloane responded. "His classes aren't done for a few weeks. I'll tell him you said hello."

"Tell him I said to come intern for me," Glenn's voice boomed. Sloane rolled her eyes. If Nico was going to do any work on a vineyard, it would be with her. "And bring this girl of yours around, too."

A thrill rushed down Sloane's spine. Blake wasn't *her girl*. But she didn't want to contradict Glenn. So, she let the words float around in the room, letting them drip down like legs on a glass of wine.

Still, Sloane couldn't help but smile as she watched Blake navigate the evening. Blake glowed with confidence, even if she didn't know a single soul in the room. She was doing her best—being polite, playing along—but there was a slight edge to her responses, a self-awareness that wasn't lost on Sloane.

Blake had a way of making everyone feel at ease while still holding on to her quiet, authentic self. And as the night wore on, Sloane noticed something else—how everyone, from the business tycoons to the local winemakers, seemed to love Blake. They asked her questions about her writing, curious about the behind-the-scenes of her career, all the while teasing her gently about her "Southern California ways" and wondering if she felt out of place among the Napa crowd.

One of the older women at the table, who had been friends with Sloane's family for years, raised an eyebrow at her. "I have to say, Sloane," she said with a knowing smile. "You two make a lovely pair. The way you look at each other—it's almost like you've been together forever."

Blake's cheeks flushed a soft pink, and she shot Sloane a quick, playful look. "Oh, we're not a couple," she said, but her voice was just a touch too defensive. "We're just friends. Old friends who found each other again."

The table erupted in knowing laughter, but there was a warmth in their teasing. It wasn't mean-spirited. It was just *comfortable*.

"I don't know," another woman chimed in. "You two certainly seem like more than just friends. Come on, Sloane, you're glowing tonight. There's something in the air, don't you think?"

Sloane's heart twisted. She hadn't noticed how hard she'd been working to suppress that quiet glow—the one that came from more than just the wine. She caught Blake's eye across the table. There was something different in the way Blake looked at her tonight. Something that made her pulse skip, that made the air between them feel charged.

But she couldn't afford to linger in that feeling. Blake was leaving in just a few days. Letting herself believe in anything beyond this week was a luxury she couldn't afford—not again.

Sloane had promised Blake her time, not her heart. She hadn't agreed to relive what it felt like to love her. And certainly not to hope.

She forced her gaze away and smoothed her expression into something neutral.

"I'm happy," Sloane said, her voice light, the words almost convincing. "It's just nice to see you all again." She added, with a teasing lilt, "But I promise, there's nothing going on here."

Even as she said it, part of her wished it were a lie.

Blake raised an eyebrow and leaned back in her chair. "Sloane's right. Just old friends with an unexpected reunion."

She held Sloane's eyes for a beat and Sloane's

pulse quickened with nervous excitement. With possibility. A small inkling that Blake was having the same confused rush of emotion as her. She didn't know what to do with the feeling, so she took another sip of wine and quickly changed the subject.

The laughter around the table picked up again, but Blake's voice, though light, had a softness to it that made Sloane's chest tighten just a little. The teasing had a warmth to it, but there was also an undercurrent of something *more*—an unspoken connection that had been simmering between them for years.

Sloane watched her, her heart swelling a little with pride. She'd always admired Blake's ability to weave a story, to make people see the world through her eyes. Tonight, in the midst of all the polished luxury, Blake was the most real thing in the room.

"So, Blake," a woman in a flowing summer dress asked, "what's the best destination you've written about? What's the one place that's stuck with you the most?"

Blake paused, considering the question. "It's tough," she said, her fingers lightly tracing the stem of her wineglass. "But I'd say one of my favorites was a small town in Positano. It wasn't on anyone's radar, but it was just *real*. The food, the people, the way everything felt untouched by the big tourist rush. It was…perfect, in its own way."

Sloane smiled softly. Blake's eyes sparkled as she talked—the genuine passion and curiosity always there. It was the thing that had drawn Sloane to her all those years ago, and it still caught her in a way she wasn't quite ready to admit.

"Remember that farmhouse?" Sloane shared the memory without thinking. "We were going to buy that place."

Blake's soft laughter seemed to reach across the table, a balm for Sloane. She remembered it, too. The dilapidated farmhouse that was supposed to become their future. "That place was a mess. But it was gorgeous. I wonder if it's still standing? And if the vineyard next to it has produced anything."

"A farmhouse in Italy? Now, that's the dream," another guest said, and Sloane could sense Blake relaxing into the conversation now, the questions and teasing fading into background noise. It wasn't so much about the place—it was about how Blake made the world feel real. She always had.

The night went on like that—lighthearted, full of laughter, and a surprising amount of warmth. As the last course, a delicate chocolate mousse with a hint of sea salt, was served, the conversation drifted into softer tones, with people talking about their favorite memories of Napa. The laughter continued, but there was an easy feeling to it now.

Blake, though still a little out of her element, had finally relaxed into the night. She sipped her wine, a half smile playing on her lips. She'd navigated the evening well, despite feeling like an outsider at first. And somehow, Sloane had the sense that Blake was *starting* to let herself enjoy this—whatever *this* was—just a little bit more than she had at the start.

And as the night wound down, with people exchanging final toasts and goodbyes, Sloane felt her gaze drift back to Blake, who was now in the middle of a lively conversation with one of the other guests. The way Blake smiled, the way she fit into this world with her own quiet charm—it made Sloane's chest ache in a way she wasn't ready to fully unpack.

But for now, she was content with just watching her—glowing, real and entirely herself.

CHAPTER SEVEN

Blake

THE COOL MORNING air drew goose bumps along Blake's arms as she followed the short path from her cottage to the entrance of the resort. The moon was still low in the sky and she was going to give Robby an earful about this early morning wake-up call—who requires guests to be up before dawn?

The itinerary had only told her to dress warm, in layers and be at the front of the resort by four thirty in the morning. She'd thrown on some jeans and a sweater over a simple shirt. Blake wasn't worried about trying to impress anyone. She was certain she was alone on this adventure, since she and Sloane hadn't talked about it.

And maybe that's why the sight of early morning Sloane caught Blake off guard when she turned the corner and saw her standing by the entrance of Vella West. She wore fitted jeans and a tight black hooded sweatshirt and a beanie. She looked younger somehow, like the girl Blake had known before. Sloane was makeup free and sipping on a white to-go cup with a brown sleeve. When she saw Blake, she stood and strode toward her with purpose, never losing eye contact.

She held out a cup and Blake took it, even though she didn't drink coffee. At least it would keep her hands warm.

"What's this?" Blake asked as she took the cup.

Sloane shrugged. "A peace offering," she said. "I hope you don't mind, but I canceled the van pickup. I—well, I would prefer to drive."

Sloane's body stiffened as she waited for Blake's response. Blake wasn't sure what had her so nervous, probably the fact that the two of them were going to be alone together.

"That's fine with me," Blake said, her voice way too chipper for a before-dawn conversation. "Are you going to tell me what we're doing?"

Sloane offered her a secret, smug smile. "Nope. It's meant to be a surprise activity, according to Robby." She tipped her head toward the passenger door of her sleek black coupe. "First, we have to get there. Then you'll see."

They drove in the gray early morning light down the winding roads in relative silence. Blake's thoughts were a swirl of confusion and excitement as she peeked at Sloane out of the corner of her eye. Various resorts hidden behind high walls and gates flew past them as Sloane drove down the highway.

"Is something wrong with your drink?" Sloane asked. The coffee sat untouched in the cup holder, seeming to taunt Blake.

"No." Blake grimaced and grabbed the cup. She prepared herself for the bitter taste of coffee. But as she took a sip, a jolt of cream and Earl Grey hit her tongue. "Oh! It's tea."

Sloane scrunched her brow in confusion. "Of course it's tea."

"You remember how I take my tea?"

"Blake, you were insufferable in the morning until you'd had at least two cups of tea. I've probably watched you drink a thousand of those. Of course I remember."

Blake let the words settle low in her belly. Like most things with Sloane, it was an ache and a soothing balm all at once. Blake smiled down at the cup. She didn't respond, but she silently drank her tea and pondered the fact that Sloane remembered.

When Sloane pulled off the highway and onto a dirt road Blake noticed a sign that read Wine Country Tours in swoopy letters. Something prickled at the back of her mind. A memory. A dream.

Slowing down, Sloane turned into a dirt parking area, revealing the scene before them. There were six different wicker baskets large enough to hold at least ten people, arranged in a field. Even in the darkness, Blake could see ribbons of color spread out behind them. A breath hitched in Blake's throat and something tightened in her chest.

"Sloane—" The words cut off in her throat. "What are we..."

Sloane parked the car and turned to look at Blake. "Come on, we don't want to be late."

When Blake was younger, she'd stare at the hot-air balloons in the early morning sky. A trip was so far outside her budget she'd never even dreamed of booking a flight. But she had told Sloane about it. One morning Sloane had woken her before dawn, a steaming mug of tea in hand and they'd driven out to an open field.

Together they'd lain in the dewdrop grass and watched as giant orbs came into view. A kaleidoscope of color across the early morning sky.

"I'm going to do that someday," Blake had whispered into her mouth. "Just float away with nothing but heat and air and silence."

"Sounds terrifying."

"Sounds amazing."

"Maybe. If you're not afraid of heights."

"Well, yes, there's that." She'd kissed Sloane and let her fingertips trail up and down her spine beneath her sweater. "Are you saying you won't go with me?"

"I'd go for you," Sloane had promised between kisses. "I'll be terrified. And panicking the entire time. But let me be there. The first time you go."

"I will." Blake had said as Sloane pushed her back on the blanket and trailed kisses down her neck. "I'll wait for you."

And she had. Blake had had opportunities to try this, but she always turned them down or found an excuse. It felt right to be here now, with an older version of Sloane. There were a million promises they'd both broken to each other over the years, but she'd kept this one.

"I thought we were doing something from my itinerary?" Blake really wanted to go on this adventure, but it felt like too much. It was too special.

"This is on your itinerary," Sloane said with a wink. "I just tweaked it a little."

Blake was still trying to decide what to do about that wink when Sloane pointed across the field. "Come on, this one is ours." Sloane tugged on Blake's sleeve and Blake felt it in her stomach.

A wicker basket, much smaller than the rest, sat in the middle of the field. "Why is it so much smaller?" Blake had researched this. There were weight limits and balance requirements. And she realized now that she was going to be in that tiny basket with Sloane and a pilot and probably a few other strangers. Nerves coiled deep in her stomach like a spring, circling tighter and tighter until she was sure she'd be sick.

As they approached the basket, a man from the night before strode over. "It's all set for you, Sloane."

"Thanks."

He held up a fist, and she bumped it. Blake stifled a giggle at the sight of Sloane fist-bumping anyone.

Then he walked away.

"You first, Miller." Sloane gestured to the basket. Blake hadn't been nervous until now. Somehow, this tiny basket was going to hold at least three people with nothing but heat. There was no way.

"But we're missing our pilot," Blake protested.

Sloane climbed over the edge of the basket and stretched out her hand to Blake. She blinked at her. "Blake, *I'm* the pilot."

Blake stared at Sloane's outstretched hand like it was some kind of trick. The balloon loomed beyond them, the burner sputtering in rhythmic bursts, and still—still—she couldn't make the pieces fit.

"*You're* the pilot?" she said again, arms folded tight across her chest.

Sloane didn't flinch. "Yes," she said simply. "I got restless a few years ago. My entire life was mapped out for me and none of it felt like it was mine. I needed something just for me. And I know we promised to do this together one day. I guess it was my way of keeping that summer alive. That sounds ridiculous. I know."

A flash of electricity ran down Blake's spine and crackled along her fingertips, but whether it was anger or awe—or that dangerous space in between—she couldn't tell. Ten years of nothing. No calls. No texts. No quick, cowardly message on social media. Just silence.

And now this?

Sloane must have spent hundreds of hours getting certified, mastering the rules, learning the language of flight, just to—what? Carry some kind of torch for Blake? Sweep back in and dazzle her with a grand gesture?

It was infuriating. It was ridiculous. It was kind of...breathtaking.

The heat rising from the burner couldn't compare to the slow burn in Blake's chest. Maybe it wasn't really about the balloon. Maybe it was about all the things Sloane hadn't said, all the time that had passed. But it was also about the way Sloane looked at her now. Steady. Unflinching. Like she wasn't afraid anymore. Like she wasn't going to run.

Blake's throat tightened. The basket creaked slightly as Sloane shifted her weight. Her hand was still there, open between them, waiting.

Blake hesitated—just long enough to feel the gravity of it. Then she reached out and took it. Warm, calloused fingers closed around hers, and something settled in her chest like the quiet before takeoff.

"Okay," Blake whispered. "Then take me."

Blake forced her feet to move forward. She climbed into the basket, marveling at the fact that Sloane had done this, for her.

Sloane

When Sloane had shown up at Wine Country Tours three years ago asking for pilot lessons, she had needed a distraction. She'd spent seven years raising her cousin, and several weeks feeling lost once he left for college. The owner had laughed at her and offered her a ride instead. But she'd showed up the next day. And then the next. Finally, he'd agreed to take her on a private flight and explain the mechanics—if she paid.

It had taken three years, lots of money and hundreds of logged hours. But Sloane had gotten her pilot's license. It was one of her most prized possessions. Something she'd worked hard for just because she'd wanted it.

It had been a promise to herself that one day she'd get back to the woman she'd been before her world had shifted in an instant. Up in the air, she wasn't a caregiver. She wasn't a billionaire by horrible, horrible circumstance. She was just Sloane.

When they were secure in the basket, the team worked with her to get the balloon full and rising. They were the first to take off, the sky still inky black as they rose slowly and steadily off the ground. Sloane hated this part. The wobble, the uncertainty, the slow progression into the air. But with Blake next to her now, it was worth it.

Blake gasped when the basket jolted and her knuckles turned white as they gripped the edge. She let out a laugh, breathless and joyful, when they were just a few feet off the ground.

"How did you manage this?" Blake asked, her voice a little breathless with disbelief. Sloane snuck a glance at her and saw her staring—not at the balloon, but at her. Really looking. "I thought you were afraid of heights?"

Sloane's fingers clamped on the handle reflexively. She was *terrified* of heights. She gave the handle a firm tug, the burner roaring to life in response.

"I am," she breathed.

The fear hadn't gone away—it never did. It still crawled up the back of her neck, made her fingers twitch just before takeoff. But she'd stopped trying to push it down. These days, it was familiar. Almost grounding. A steady reminder that some things were worth doing scared.

"Can I do that?" Blake leaned in, eyes following the line from Sloane's hand to the mouth of the balloon above them, bright and impossibly open against the sky.

"Technically? No. But, here." Sloane reached out her hand and pulled Blake closer. Up close, she smelled like rosewater and lavender. Like ten years hadn't passed. Blake's hair swirled around her, falling into her eyes. Sloane should have told her to wear a hat. She brushed Blake's hair off her cheek and Blake's breath hitched.

"Hold here," Sloane instructed.

Blake grasped the handle, and a bubble of laughter escaped her soft lips. Sloane gripped Blake's hip and held her steady. The air was cooler up here, the heat from the balloon kept them slightly warmer. But the heat pooling in Sloane's belly made the basket feel like an inferno.

"Okay, pull now." Sloane wrapped her fingers around Blake's and they pulled down. The fire burned bright above them and then there was a steady tug, like the earth going out from underneath her feet, as they lifted higher in the air.

"Sloane, this is amazing," Blake whispered. The sun melted over the horizon, spreading out like a layer of honey. The air came alive around them with mist and the promise of dew on the vines. Several hot-air balloons stretched across the sky in a patchwork quilt of color. Sloane wasn't one to take pictures. But she wished she was, just to capture the way Blake's chestnut curls whipped in the wind.

Sloane wanted to whisper all the things she hadn't been able to say. Maybe up here, where the world was silent and the ground was vineyards and hills and homes that looked more like pointillism than real life, she could say all the things she regretted. She should have called. Or that she sometimes typed Blake Miller into Google but never hit Search. Perhaps her greatest regret was not knowing how Blake had gotten a small scar on the knuckle of her ring finger. How many other things had Sloane missed?

"I know," she said instead, staring at the slope of Blake's neck where it dipped into her sweater.

"I want more of this, I think," Blake went on. "I've spent the last ten years in an office. I want to *live*. I want to travel and see the world again. Do you miss it?"

Sloane swallowed. She did miss it. And she

didn't. She missed feeling like she didn't have a care in the world. And she also loved her cousin more than any stamp in her passport. "Sometimes," she said gently. "Sometimes."

"Can we see the resort from here?" Blake asked. She leaned over the basket and Sloane reached out to pull her back in on instinct. Blake's body fell flush against Sloane's with a thud.

"Easy there," Sloane laughed. "You need to keep your arms and legs inside at all times."

Blake nodded and pressed her body closer. Sloane allowed herself a moment to feel the weight of Blake's body before she inevitably pulled away.

"Over there." Sloane gestured east, and just at the base of a hill. The resort lay out like a map. The main house, the cottages, the stables. And the vineyards. The first time Sloane had seen it like this, it was still under renovations.

"Wow," Blake breathed. "It looks so small. How many times have you done this?"

"Too many times to count." Sloane smiled at Blake. Blake's eyes went soft.

"So, this is what you've been up to? Learning to fly?"

She said the words teasingly, but there was an edge to it. "Yup."

Blake had a million questions for Sloane as

she took photographs of the world below. And she asked every single one. *How high would they go? How were they going to land?*

She leaned forward, rested her chin on Blake's shoulder and pointed. "We'll probably land somewhere over there." Blake followed her fingers to a light green patch of land. She nodded once, then snapped a photo before turning the camera on Sloane.

"May I?" she asked. She looked up at Sloane, a question in her eyes. Sloane nodded and pretended not to see the camera as Blake snapped a few more photos of them. Sloane's throat felt tight, wondering if every emotion showed on her face.

Because having Blake this close felt *right.* And she wasn't ready to come down from this moment.

CHAPTER EIGHT

Blake

AN HOUR HAD passed since the balloon had touched down in an enormous field somewhere in another county, yet Blake's thoughts remained suspended among the clouds. It had felt so right to have Sloane's arms around her, keeping her safe. And that terrified her.

She knew spending time with Sloane in any capacity would be tricky. Too many old feelings and old hurts to keep hidden behind polite conversations. But she hadn't expected the overwhelming surge of emotions that would follow, like a rushing river she couldn't contain inside the banks. Sloane had a way of infiltrating her mind and heart, blurring the lines between professional and past. Blake realized that had she declined Sloane's invitation and attended these events alone, she would have been the third wheel in some group, laughing and boarding a van to return to the resort.

Which would have been fine.

But she *wasn't* alone. She was with Sloane. Confident, poised and effortlessly charming Sloane Vella, who had dismissed the van caravan that was supposed to bring them back to Napa and assured Blake that a car would come for them later. With a nod, the van driver handed Blake a wicker basket with a blanket on top.

"What's all this?" Blake inquired, eyeing the basket as if it were a wild animal.

Sloane smiled. "I didn't have a chance to eat breakfast and thought we might be hungry after the flight."

Blake's heart tightened at the memory of Sloane always packing a small snack during their early morning hikes or train rides across Europe. She had always insisted it was for herself, yet would share with Blake when her stomach inevitably rumbled two hours into their adventure.

Blake rolled her eyes, suppressing the memory. She didn't need to get wrapped up in her better memories of Sloane. Or how they contrasted with her lavish displays this week. These elaborate gestures were simply a flashy display of wealth and privilege—or maybe they were just Sloane's way of controlling the narrative.

After all, Sloane was here to ensure Blake wrote a glowing review.

Despite her insistence on Blake's impartiality, she had arranged a private hot-air balloon ride for the two of them and was now spreading a thick blanket in the middle of an empty field. A gentle breeze stirred around them, and if Blake squinted, she could almost picture herself at twenty-two, two hundred dollars to her name and a single backpack full of her life's contents.

She needed to get ahold of herself.

"Well, this certainly beats cheap granola bars and a shared bottle of sparkling water," Blake laughed breathlessly as she sat on the blanket.

"I don't know," Sloane replied, sitting beside her. She opened the basket and began unpacking the food. "I kind of liked those adventures."

Blake swallowed thickly. She didn't want to admit that she had enjoyed them, too. Because then she'd have to acknowledge how much it hurt to have it all taken away. How she had struggled to exchange her ticket and fly home alone, shattered, when Sloane had disappeared.

"Yeah, me too."

They sat in silence for a few moments. The sun crested the hill, casting a soft glow around them. Golden light caught the edges of Sloane's hair as she reached forward and plucked a strawberry from the wooden board.

"So," Blake said slowly, carefully, "did you always want to open a resort? I don't remember you mentioning it."

Sloane sighed. "Sort of. This was all my uncle's before he passed away. His name. His legacy. His fields. And I'm honored to continue his work. But the resort is my chance to do something I've dreamed up. And I want to make sure I get it right."

"Oh, Sloane. I'm so sorry." Her fingers twitched with the desire to touch Sloane. To hug her or comfort her somehow. But nerves held her back.

Something that resembled heartache crossed Sloane's face for just a moment. "It was a long time ago. But I'm not like you. I didn't get to pursue my dreams. I inherited someone else's. And it's my duty to make it right."

Blake had to stifle a scoff. Sloane had no idea what she was talking about. "I don't know that I'd call my job a dream. I create social media posts. I pitch ideas. This is my first assignment. I'm not a writer. Not anymore."

"You *are* a writer. You know that, right?"

Sloane touched Blake's wrist, and she felt it everywhere. How could the brush of Sloane's steady, thin fingers leave a trail of goose bumps on contact?

"I've always loved your words."

"You knew me for two months, Sloane. A lot has changed since then. You wouldn't even recognize my writing now. It's all hashtags and clickbait headlines."

That was a lie. Even though they'd only spent two months together, the connection they shared was something Blake hadn't felt with anyone since. She didn't believe in fate, not really. Soulmates? Definitely not. But if she ever were to believe, it would be because of Sloane.

From the moment their eyes met on that quiet, half-forgotten beach—both of them wandering, lost in different ways—Blake had felt something shift. She'd known. Or at least, she thought she had.

Within a week, they were inseparable. Their hearts and hands had tangled so tightly, Blake wasn't sure she'd ever fully untie the tethers they'd formed.

Sloane reached out again, gently brushing a strand of hair from Blake's face. Heat flared—down Blake's neck, across her collarbones, and curled low in her belly. Sloane's touch shouldn't be able to do that. Not after all this time. But, somehow, it could. Blake forced her eyes closed to fight against her desire to lean into the touch.

"I'd know your words anywhere," Sloane whispered. "I must have memorized every word you wrote that summer. I still have one of your notebooks—pages full of your doodles, half-formed verses, lines you tossed aside like they were nothing. It wound up in my bag and I didn't notice until I unpacked a month later."

"Well, I'm going to need that back," Blake said. She tried to push calm into her voice, but it still came out breathy. All the while, her heart beat rapidly at the revelation.

Sloane hadn't forgotten her. Not completely.

"Sure." Sloane gave her a lopsided smile and continued. "I whisper them to the vines sometimes, when they need some encouragement. Your words, Blake. They've carried me through…more than you can imagine. So don't tell me you're not the same. Even if you've changed—I still know you."

"Don't do that," Blake practically growled. "I'm supposed to be mad at you." Blake was mad. At least, she had been. Sloane had left her on read for nearly a decade. While she was, what, building an empire? But her touch combined with that confession made Blake weak. Sloane had saved her journal. She'd memorized her words. She saw her for who she really was. And it hurt.

"You can," Sloane breathed. "You can be mad." She tucked a strand of Blake's hair behind her ear. Sloane's fingertips on the shell of her ear sent fire coursing through her once again. "I'd be mad at me," Sloane whispered.

Blake's emotions clawed at her throat and rose up in pinpricks across her skin. She blinked rapidly. She wanted to storm off this blanket; she wanted to lay Sloane bare; she wanted to demand Sloane tell her why she hadn't called.

But one look into Sloane's wide, midnight-dark eyes made her question everything. This woman had endured the loss of her uncle, rescued a failing winery, built a resort from the ground up. She carried the weight of it all with quiet strength. Blake might've been angry, but she was also in awe. She wanted to pull Sloane close, to give her a place to rest—somewhere she didn't have to pretend.

Any chance Blake thought she had of staying strong fell away on the breeze like white puffs of dandelion spores. She leaned forward and pressed a soft kiss to the edge of Sloane's mouth, just to keep her from talking. It was barely the breath of a kiss. Not even a whisper. Still, Blake felt it in her toes.

Sloane froze, and Blake worried she'd made a terrible mistake. Maybe she'd misread the romantic balloon ride, the flowers, the champagne, and the sweet fruit bursting on her tongue. But then Sloane turned her head and opened her mouth to the kiss.

Sloane

Blake still tasted the same. Like Earl Gray and the hint of mint, and she smelled like a garden—

rose and lavender and all of Sloane's better memories. She needed to catch her breath. She wanted to tell Blake everything.

She *should* tell Blake everything—about her cousin and her family obligations. But first, she kissed Blake tenderly, slowing down their frantic kisses to a measured dance. Blake kissed Sloane like she wanted to steal the secrets out of her. Sloane kissed Blake back like she needed Blake to know exactly why she couldn't.

When Blake tugged gently at Sloane's lower lip, it stung, but Sloane leaned down and into it, giving Blake exactly what she wanted.

She slid her body down next to Blake's on the blanket, fingers threading through the tangled curls now a mess from the wind and their frantic kisses. Her hands traced slow, featherlight paths over Blake's shoulder, then down her arm, lingering at the curve of her hip before ghosting over the swell of her breasts. Blake melted into the touch, nuzzling against Sloane's palm, pressing softly as if seeking to hold on to this moment before it slipped away.

Sloane loved that she knew how to tame the fire in Blake. They'd been through this before. She remembered how to talk her down, how to listen without judgment. Now she just hoped Blake could do the same for her.

But first, Sloane needed to steady her own

breathing. She pulled away, just enough to clear her head. Sloane rubbed her thumb along the inside of Blake's wrist—back and forth, slow and soothing—until their breathing softened and the frantic energy between them mellowed.

"I'm sorry." Blake's cheeks flushed pink in the early morning sun. "I shouldn't have just kissed you like that. It won't happen again."

"Is that what you think?" Sloane asked, voice teasing. "That I'm mad you kissed me?"

Blake tried to look above her head at the wrists Sloane held gently but firmly. "Um, yes?"

Sloane chuckled softly, releasing Blake's wrists. The sudden absence of Blake's skin made Sloane ache in a way she hadn't expected. A way she shouldn't want.

"I don't regret kissing you," Sloane said warily. "I meant what I said. It's okay to be mad at me. It was awful of me to disappear on you. And I can't begin to tell you how sorry I am. I never should have left you alone, with only a note."

Blake sat up, frowning slightly. "Okay, yeah. I just got overwhelmed. This blanket, the breakfast… It feels like we're back in—"

"Sorrento." They said it simultaneously, then Blake laughed.

"I know, right?"

"I loved that place," Blake said, pressing her palms to her cheeks. "But we aren't there. I need to stay focused this week. I can't afford any distractions." Blake trailed off, the weight of responsibility seeming to settle over her.

Sloane nodded. "I understand." She was letting her fantasies run wild, but Blake was here on business. Sloane was trying to—maybe not win her back—but make amends somehow. She wanted to make sure they left this week on better terms. Maybe after all this, they could walk away not as friends, but at least not strangers.

Her phone chimed. She ignored it. Then it beeped again. It could be their driver. Sloane peeked and saw Nico's name flash. She sent him to voicemail and hoped he was okay. She'd call him back soon.

"Everything okay?" Blake asked.

"Yeah. My…cousin. I'll call him back."

"You have a cousin?" Blake said softly, mostly to herself. "There's so much I don't know about you."

"Hey, it's okay. Look at me." Blake didn't look up. Sloane tried again, softer. "We have a few days together. So, we got caught up in memories. It doesn't have to happen again. And we don't have to be embarrassed about it. I just know I had no idea how much I missed you until I saw you in the lobby two days ago."

Understatement of the year.

Blake snorted.

"And, you said so yourself—you need to write a review that will impress your boss. Which means you need to keep doing the resort's planned events."

"You're telling me this hot-air balloon ride was a resort event? Do you take all your guests on private rides?"

"Okay, fine. This one I got a little carried away with. A hot-air balloon ride was on the agenda—I just wasn't the pilot. But trust me, you don't want to see me as a bystander on one of those things. I'm much better when I'm in control."

"Yeah, you are." Blake blushed fiercely. "Oh my gosh, I said that out loud. See? See what you do?"

Sloane smiled wide. She adored seeing her so flustered, so alive. She loved Blake like this. No—not loved. What a silly word to pop into her mind. Sloane was careful, she had people depending on her. Nico, and Robby and the entire community. Feelings led to distractions. And distractions led to heartache and tragedy. She wasn't going to go there again.

"Blake." She said her name like a warning. Maybe for herself.

"So, what? We just keep doing these events and pretend this never happened?" Blake asked, raising an eyebrow.

Sloane sighed. “Well, I don’t know that I’ll be very good at that.”

As if on cue, the crunch of gravel announced two cars approaching nearby. Sloane smiled at the sight of her sleek black coupe. Robby emerged, a giant cup of coffee in hand, their expression more scowl than smile. Sloane was going to have some explaining to do.

She waved. Robby nodded once before jumping into the waiting town car.

“I’m sorry. Did Robby just drop off your car so we can drive back?”

Sloane hadn’t considered how it looked. She didn’t get in cars with others. She couldn’t tell Blake that. So, she said, “Yes. As a favor. They’re not just the head of PR. They’re kind of my only friend these days. Besides, I, um, don’t get in cars with other people driving. And Robby knows that.”

Robby truly was a good friend. Sloane had a panic attack the first and only time she’d tried to let someone else drive. Her uncle’s death made it impossible for her to trust others behind the wheel. Robby had helped her through it. She’d avoid driving altogether if she could.

“Does that mean we need to leave?” Blake looked around the field as if suddenly realizing where they were.

"No, Blake. We don't have to leave. Not yet. We can stay as long as you want."

She flopped back on the blanket. "I'd like that."

Her sweater rode up slightly, exposing a sliver of skin at her waist, and Sloane groaned, looking away to hide her reaction.

"I missed you," Blake murmured. "I'm still mad at you. But I missed you. I'm glad you're okay. I'm glad I ran into you like this. Even if it still hurts a little."

Sloane's chest swelled with regret and frustration. Guilt and grief warred inside her. She thought she might cry. And Sloane didn't cry.

"I missed you, too," she finally admitted.

Blake picked up a muffin, breaking it in half. She offered the larger piece to Sloane, who took it tentatively.

"Here. Muffin peace offering."

Sloane scrunched her brows in confusion. "Is that a thing?"

"I think so. I'm pretty sure. Now we don't get to be angry anymore. We just get carbs."

Sloane's laughter rang out—big, bright and contagious. Blake snorted, nudging Sloane playfully, which only made her laugh harder. Within minutes, they dissolved into giggles. Blake wiped at her eyes and Sloane offered a napkin.

"You could always make me laugh," Sloane said.

"No, it's not me. It's us. The two of us together.

Can we just have more of this?" Blake's voice softened, careful. "I'm tired of being angry. I don't want the hurt to take over the time we have. I just… I want to pause it. Just for a bit."

Sloane swallowed hard. Saying yes should have been easy. But nothing between them had been simple in a long time.

She didn't answer immediately. Instead, she reached out slowly, tucking a loose strand of hair behind Blake's ear. Her hand lingered longer than it should have—as if afraid the moment might vanish if she let go too quickly.

"I'd like that," she whispered, voice low and steady as the breeze weaving through the field.

She reached for Blake's hand, not with the certainty she once had, but with a tentative, hopeful question. Their palms met, fingers intertwining—both familiar and new all at once. The kind of touch that remembers what was, and aches for what might be again.

Sloane went still, forehead dipping to rest gently against Blake's. Having her this close felt like something good she didn't deserve. Something she hadn't felt in a very, very long time.

Blake's breath caught and she pulled her fingers away. She took a small bite of muffin and chewed thoughtfully. "Okay, Sloane. This muffin is surprisingly good." Her eyes glinted with mirth. "Now, I *know* you didn't make it."

A derisive scoff that was awfully close to laughter escaped Sloane's lips as Blake playfully shoved her, their glee echoing in the air. It seemed Blake remembered everything, too. Down to the fact that the only thing Sloane could make was tea.

Sloane didn't know if that meant forgiveness—or simply that Blake couldn't bear to fight anymore. Sloane would worry about that bit later.

CHAPTER NINE

Blake

BLAKE WASN'T SURE what had overwhelmed her in that field—the sudden rush of feeling, the way her hand had caressed Sloane's cheek as if it was the only natural thing in the world. The kiss had caught her off guard, yet somehow, it was exactly what she needed. She hadn't realized how deeply she'd missed Sloane until she felt that pressure loosen and then swell again in her chest.

Being near her made everything else—the uncertainty, the weight of the past ten years—fade into a strange kind of lightness. Like a hot-air balloon slowly lifting inside her, expanding and carrying her somewhere higher, further than she'd been willing to go before. She was dizzy with it, nearly drunk on the sensation.

Now, alone in her room, the gauzy curtains stirred in the soft afternoon breeze drifting in from the southern-facing porch. Blake tried to imagine her life with Sloane back in it. How would they even begin to merge their lives?

Blake had worked too hard and for too long to move on from Sloane. She was really good at ignoring the ache in her chest whenever she saw a woman with sleek black hair or heard a laugh that was both soft and confident. Blake was just beginning to get back out there. She was ready to travel again. She was ready to prove to Tara (and to herself) that she was a professional writer.

As if on cue, Blake's phone buzzed rhythmically on the desk, yanking her from the moment in the field and back into the present. The screen lit up with another message from Chloe. Please send pages or notes. Tara is downing fistfuls of antacids and angry typing. Maybe she'll calm down if she hears from you. You can do this.

Blake bit her lip, hesitating. She and Chloe had become friends over the past few years. This wasn't just a friendly reminder—this was a warning from a friend. She needed to get something to Tara as a sign of good faith.

There was just one problem.

She had no pages, no neat notes—only scraps and half-formed ideas she already hated. Panic crept up the back of her throat. What if Tara hated everything she sent? Would Tara fire her mid-trip?

Maybe.

But she *was* a writer. That much Sloane had reminded her of just this morning, lying together on that blanket in the sun. The way Sloane had pulled that part of her up from somewhere buried deep, kissed it awake until it fluttered around them like something alive and urgent. Blake was a writer. She could do this. She had to.

She tapped out a quick message promising notes would come, then grabbed her pen and old, worn notebook. Sliding onto the chaise lounge on the balcony, she sank into its soft cushions, feeling the warm afternoon sun on her skin and breathing in the faint scent of jasmine carried on the wind.

The blank page stared up at her, daunting and open. What could she say? Half of her experiences so far felt like private moments, not something fit for a travel magazine. Writing it all down felt like exposing a secret that wasn't hers to tell. Maybe she'd invent a story about having a partner for this trip. None of the readers would know. But that felt disingenuous and not at all how she wanted to start her career.

Besides, she didn't want to do that to Sloane.

This morning, Sloane had been there, real and undeniable. The way the sunlight had danced in her hair, the quiet courage in her eyes, the way she'd reached for Blake's hand like it was the only anchor she had. Sloane was the reason everything had felt so perfect—so achingly perfect—even if she'd vanished the moment they returned to the resort, all mysterious and secretive about some urgent work.

A cold wash of reality settled over Blake, sharp and unwelcome. She knew Sloane was the owner of this place. Surely there were a thousand things for her to do. She didn't have time for horseback rides and hot-air balloon dates. Still, the fear squeezed her ribs, heavy and relentless. The sun sank lower beyond the hills, casting sharp shadows across the page and her thoughts. There was no one to tell this to, no one who understood this particular ache.

So, Blake let the words spill onto the page instead. She didn't censor herself. She didn't think of Tara, or the magazine or the careful professionalism she was supposed to maintain. She simply wrote—her frustrations, her hopes, the stinging loneliness she'd felt when Sloane had slipped away that morning. And how it mirrored the pain she'd felt ten years ago.

She wrote about the way she'd left behind the girl she used to be, the dreams and plans she'd had by the Italian seashore, ten years ago. How she'd come home a ghost of herself, resigned to believing the best years were long gone.

The pen scratched across the pages, sometimes fast and breathless, sometimes halting and unsure. For over an hour she poured out fragments of herself, messy and raw—some illegible, some surprisingly clear. Maybe this was just a jumble of ramblings; maybe one day it could become something. Maybe it would fade into nothing. But in that moment, Blake felt alive in a way she hadn't dared feel in years. The part of her that had gone silent was waking up, groggy and disoriented, but unmistakably present.

When she finally paused, she stretched her fingers and cracked her neck, the weight in her chest still lingering. She stared down at the pages filled with her tangled thoughts. She couldn't use them—not yet—but a warmth expanded in her chest at the relief of just getting it out. The words were hers to keep, to protect, to maybe one day share.

Her phone rang this time. Blake answered it without looking, still lost in the daze of getting words to the page. "Hello?" she said absently.

"Blake!" Chloe's whispered screech made Blake's stomach flip. "Words. Now. Your social media posts are great, but they aren't calming Tara down. If anything, they're having the opposite effect."

Blake swallowed thickly. Her posts had garnered thousands of likes. Especially the one she'd uploaded this morning with a view of the resort from above. "What do you mean? They're doing well."

"Exactly," hissed Chloe. "Don't remind her you're good at social media. Show her you are also a *writer.* Send her something to prove you can write this story."

"I'm on it," Blake lied. She glanced at her notebook, full of things she'd never print. "Five minutes. Stall her for me?"

"You got it," Chloe said with relief in her voice. "Five minutes."

The line went silent with static air. There was work to do. She opened her laptop this time and began writing again—this time with clarity and purpose. She described the resort in vivid detail, capturing the glamor, the rustic charm, the essence of a place that felt almost magical. It was honest, straightforward—the kind of writing her editor expected. And maybe, just maybe, it was a way to hold on to the day, the fleeting peace she'd found.

She didn't mention Sloane. Not the picnic, not the way her presence had changed everything. But as Blake shared the document with Tara and Chloe, she whispered quietly to herself, "Stay focused, Miller. Be professional."

Sloane

The large mahogany desk in the middle of the room had belonged to her uncle, even though

Sloane was the one sitting behind it now. The room was a blend of old-world charm and modern elegance, with polished oak beams crisscrossing the ceiling and her mahogany desk cluttered with last-minute details. She'd let the designers have control of this space, thinking she could trust them. But it felt more like an homage to her uncle and less like her. As if the pressure of his legacy wasn't enough on its own.

Still, she loved the space. Through the tall windows, she could see the lush gardens below, dotted with guests enjoying the resort's amenities. To the left she could make out the stables beyond the luxurious cottages and the main resort's rooms.

Her phone buzzed, and she sighed, rubbing her temples before answering the FaceTime call. Nico's face appeared on the screen, his unshaved jaw and sleepy eyes a stark contrast to her polished appearance.

"Hey, kiddo," she greeted, forcing a bright note into her voice.

"Finally! What took you so long?" Nico's voice came through lively, a hint of playful impatience threading through. His lopsided grin filled the screen, his hair the mess of a college student who had just woken up mid-day.

Sloane straightened, brushing a stray strand of hair behind her ear as she shifted her weight on the leather chair. "I picked up on the second ring, thank you very much."

"Yeah, this time," he laughed. "I've been blowing up your phone for two days."

Her gaze drifted to the window for a moment, watching a group of guests laughing as they drifted by the pool. "Sorry, it's been busy around here," she admitted, glancing back at her cluttered desk, papers still waiting to be signed.

Nico's eyes narrowed slightly, his brow furrowing as he studied her face on the screen. "You look…different," he said, his tone shifting from playful to concerned. "Not bad, just… I don't know. Distracted? Flustered? What's going on?"

Sloane froze, her fingers stilling over the tablet she had been idly tapping. She hadn't realized how much her emotions were showing. Nico might be younger than her, but over the years, he'd taken care of her as much as she'd cared for him.

Both Nico and Sloane had expected her parents to get guardianship of Nico—and as a result—oversight of his trust. But Sloane's uncle surprised everyone when he left Nico, and everything else, to her. Her parents were furious, but when Nico told her he was pansexual, it made sense. Her own parents had been less than kind when she came out her freshman year of high school as a lesbian. Her uncle had been her safe haven, taking her in for the summers and loving her unconditionally. She was honored to do the same for Nico for all these years.

She forced a smile, trying to brush it off. "It's just the stress, you know? Big weekend ahead."

Nico didn't buy it. "Come on, Sloane. You're my cousin. I know when you're hiding something. What's going on?"

She sighed, leaning back in her chair, her eyes momentarily closing as she gathered her thoughts. She couldn't tell him about Blake. "It's just…everything's coming together, but it's a lot. I want this to be perfect."

Nico nodded, his expression softening. "It will be. It has to be." Nico shifted and held up his laptop. Sloane couldn't quite make out the words on the screen. "Because, I have news. I got it, Sloane. Look, the internship. I leave as soon as school's out."

Sloane's heart swelled with pride and cracked with nerves at the same time. An internship. In Italy. She'd helped him with the application. An entire summer learning about viticulture.

"Nico, oh my gosh, congratulations!" She kept her voice bright. An entire summer with him gone. He was twenty-two now. Next year he'd be graduating from college. He wasn't her baby cousin anymore. But Italy was half a world away. "I'm so happy for you!"

"Thanks," he said. He dropped the laptop with a thud onto his bed, his shoulders rising in a mixture of pride and embarrassment. "Anyway, I thought I'd come up. To celebrate."

She cleared her throat and folded her hands neatly on the desk, trying to pivot back to the weight of the conversation. "Nico…you know I want you here, but this weekend is going to be really busy. I won't have a minute to celebrate with you."

A pause lingered on the line, Nico's face softening, the excitement settling into something more thoughtful. "Fine…but soon? I want the full tour."

She smiled, reaching out to tuck a strand of hair behind her ear again, trying to steady her racing heart. "Okay, come next weekend. I promise. You'll get the full VIP treatment—and actual time with me."

"Deal. Just…try to have some fun this weekend, okay? Don't give me a reason to come up there!"

They said their goodbyes and Sloane sat back, eyes drifting again toward the window, feeling the overwhelming weight of everything—her uncle's legacy, her duties to Nico, the resort and the fragile hope she still held for herself.

But beneath it all was the niggling feeling that Blake Miller had shown up for a reason. Maybe fate had brought her here to remind Sloane that she had a life once, a life separate from raising her cousin, and saving a winery and taking on way more pressure and responsibility than she was ready for at twenty-two.

Blake's mere presence made Sloane want to try again. But that was very dangerous. Everything was riding on this week. Blake's positive review of the resort was going to launch Vella West into the world of luxury resorts. That, in turn, would increase the visibility of Vella West Vineyards. It was part of her next ten-year plan. Nico was counting on her. Robby was counting on her. Her entire staff was counting on her.

Sloane felt the pressure on her shoulders every day. A weight growing heavier and heavier as they led up to the grand opening party this weekend. Saturday night would be the lynch pin. If she could get through that night, then everything else would go into motion.

Sloane closed her eyes and rubbed at her temples, trying to forget the way it felt to have Blake next to her on that blanket. Despite the rational part of her brain screaming at her that it was impossible, Sloane desperately wanted to do it again.

CHAPTER TEN

Blake

THE GENTLE MURMUR of voices swirled in the air as Blake made her way toward the festivities the following evening. She wasn't sure what to expect. The itinerary had only said to dress in layers, bring a sweet tooth and leave your phone in the room.

She really hoped she wasn't in for some kind of cooking class or trivia challenge. But just east of the pool was an open area transformed into a cozy, romantic spot. It was all wood smoke and sugar in the air, with the glow of eight different fire pits, flickering in the growing twilight.

The staff had set out s'mores stations, complete with several kinds of gourmet chocolate and a smattering of different graham crackers, cookies and biscuits. There were long skewers and a variety of freshly made marshmallows in different flavors to choose from. The gourmet and luxurious upgrade of her beloved camping pastime from when she was a young girl made her heart all gooey like the marshmallows she intended to devour.

At the edge of the pavilion, musicians played acoustic guitars with familiar renditions of classic songs. It was one of Blake's best memories come to life, yet again.

Well, almost. She hadn't heard from Sloane all day. Which was fine. Sloane had a multimillion-dollar resort to keep afloat.

And she shouldn't have assumed Sloane would show up. Maybe it would have been worse if she did. All the couples around the firepits seemed so cozy, cuddled up together and being generally adorable. Blake wasn't sure she was ready to roast marshmallows with Sloane like they didn't still have a million things to discuss. She lingered by the food station, selecting a fluffy strawberry marshmallow encrusted with tiny fuchsia sugar crystals.

She could roast it, but it looked so inviting and sweet she shoved it into her mouth, letting the hard granules of sugar dissolve on her tongue.

"There you are, Blake." Robby's voice grew louder as they moved into Blake's line of sight. They dressed impeccably and offered Blake a genuine smiled when they realized her mouth was full of marshmallow. "How are you enjoying the evening?"

She chewed quickly, heat creeping up her cheeks. A mouth full of sticky marshmallow was no way to greet the head of PR. "Oh, it's lovely," she mumbled. Robby looked at her with a knowing smile.

"May I?" they asked. Before she could respond, they led her to a luxurious outdoor seating area and sat down next to her. They brushed at their pants to ensure there were no wrinkles. Robby cleared their throat and turned slightly toward Blake. "I hope I'm not overstepping when I say that I know you and Sloane have some kind of history together and I'm sure it was very awkward to show up here and find…her."

Heat bloomed on Blake's cheeks. "Oh, no, we're not. I mean—"

"Blake, Sloane and I are friends. It's okay. And I know she's doing everything she can to make this week as comfortable as possible for you, but I am still the PR manager. Anything you need, I'm here."

"I appreciate that, Robby. But really, we're just catching up. And since I don't have a guest with me, she's agreed to do some events with me."

Robby raised one brow with an air of amusement. "Well, that's very…nice…of her. Is she coming tonight?" Robby looked around as if Sloane was off grabbing more marshmallows.

"I have no idea," Blake answered honestly.

The weight of the words pressed on her, making her stomach turn. “I’ve spent most of the day writing. I got sort of lost in my words.”

“Working on the article?” Robby adjusted their sleeves and looked anywhere besides Blake’s eyes. They seemed to keep a quiet composure, but under the surface, Blake sensed they were nervous. “You know what, never mind. The article is none of my business.”

She needed to let them out of this conversation.

“You know, I think I’ve had enough firepit for tonight. I’m going to go for a walk and then head to bed.” After a second, she added, “The bed is super comfortable.” And then she cringed. *Now who is being awkward?*

“This also might be none of my business, but—I hear it’s gorgeous down by the stables this time of night,” Robby said softly. “At least that’s what Sloane always says.”

“Oh,” Blake said. Her voice wobbled with embarrassment. Or maybe hope. Perhaps her heart had always known its destination for the evening.

They offered her a knowing smile. “Anyway, I’m off to check on other guests. And please, let me know if there’s anything you need.” They stood and handed Blake a thin blanket draped over the arm of an Adirondack chair.

"In case you get cold. I don't like the look of those clouds."

The path to the stables was lit with tiny hidden lights, making the California poppies burst to life like fireflies lighting her way. The cool air, along with the smells of grapevines and earth, made her feel at ease. There was something about this place that made her want to carry her journal around with her and write until she ran out of ink. She wanted to commit it to memory.

Gray clouds gathered as she walked the path, and gratitude washed over her when she saw the barn in the distance. It was quiet down here. Blake reveled in the absolute stillness around her. She knew she was technically still on resort premises, but down here it all felt a million miles away. She ran her fingers along the edge of the railing that kept the horses corralled, the wood rough and steady beneath her fingertips.

How much of Sloane was in this setting? Did she design it herself? Blake couldn't help but let her thoughts drift to Sloane as she walked along the path. Maybe she shouldn't be thinking about that summer. Or yesterday morning. Or the way Sloane's hand had trailed up and down her spine like she knew her. Like they fit together perfectly.

Except they didn't. They couldn't. Not when Blake didn't know the whole story. Blake was going to find Sloane and she was going to ask for the truth. She was going to tell Sloane she needed to know why she'd left so suddenly ten years before. It would have taken two minutes to wake her up. Blake could have gone with her. Something. Anything.

Blake needed to know why she hadn't written, hadn't called, hadn't bothered to look her up *once* in the last ten years. She felt like she was losing her mind. Sloane was trying to pretend like nothing had changed.

But everything had changed.

Robby might be trying to bring them together, but they clearly didn't know the whole story. And if Sloane didn't want to tell her, after all this, then she would be okay. She could still write this story. She could still do the article. But whatever else was blooming between them would need to end.

Even if it hurt.

Blake turned in a circle, suddenly aware that the sun was beyond the hills and the lights from the resort didn't travel all the way down this path. She felt a raindrop on the back of her neck. And then another.

Out of the corner of her eye, a lamp flickered on behind the curtains of the tiny cottage—the same one she and Sloane had been in just the day before. The sight tugged at her, pulling her toward the house like a tide she couldn't resist.

Maybe this was her chance. A chance to get some answers. To see if Sloane was finally ready to talk.

Blake's heart kicked up. She was terrified Sloane would turn her away.

But at least then she'd know.

Sloane

The kettle rumbled with the beginnings of a whistle as Sloane clicked on her desk lamp. She tilted her neck to one side then the other, trying to work out the knot that had been between her shoulders since the call with her cousin.

Sloane never lied to Nico. Or told him to stay away. But Blake had crawled back under Sloane's skin messing everything up. From the moment she'd shown up in the lobby Sloane hadn't been able to think. And Nico would realize something was different if he showed up.

Thick rain drops splattered against the windowpane. Sloane ensured the window was closed and said a silent prayer that the outdoor events for the evening had wrapped up. What was it tonight? *Firepits.* Sloane closed her eyes and cursed under her breath. She had planned to surprise Blake, but she'd gotten too wrapped up in piles of paperwork.

She dropped into her chair and stared at the pictures framed on her desk. There was one of her with her parents (something she couldn't bear to throw out), a black-and-white photo strip of Sloane and Blake when they were at a fair in France (which she'd held in her hands so many times over the years Nico finally framed it for her), and one of her and Nico from fifteen years ago. When he was still a little kid and she was a moody high schooler.

She'd been staying with them for the summer, the way she had every summer since she was just a kid, and he was sticky with a popsicle dripping down his chin and she was laughing with her eyes closed.

Her uncle and Nico had been a safe space when her parents didn't even want to try to understand her. They'd spend their summers learning the language of vines and the earth, scattering wildflower seeds and singing classic rock. She remembered that day like it was yesterday. Bunches of grapes on the vine, dirt under her fingernails and love.

And now Nico was in college, older than she had been in the photo, and he still had her whole heart. She still worried about him. She'd still do anything for him. *Everything* for him.

She switched off the kettle and began her routine of making evening tea. It was the one pattern that hadn't changed for her in the last fifteen years. Peppermint tea, a book and ten minutes to herself. It didn't matter if she was traveling or working on the road, tucked away in city apartment or wrapped under an old quilt in this tiny home that felt more hers than anything else in the world. Ten minutes, peppermint tea and some deep breaths. Then she could go on.

She'd fix things with her cousin as soon as this week was done. She'd bring him up and they'd ride Winnie and Rhett and everything would be okay. Except, Sloane knew that wasn't true. Yes, she could fix things with Nico. But Blake's presence this week was rewiring Sloane. She'd never be the same after this. She wasn't going to be able to move on twice.

Maybe she shouldn't have kissed Blake on that blanket. She had wanted to. When Blake's hand brushed centimeters from her mouth, the air crackled with unspoken desire, and all it took was a slight turn of her head to press a kiss into the edge of her mouth.

It had been a terrible idea.

Hell, she probably shouldn't have taken her in the hot-air balloon to begin with. But Blake Miller had a way of turning Sloane inside out and making her want to do anything, *anything* to see her smile.

She had just taken her first sip of tea, the warm peppermint filling her nostrils with steam, when three knocks reverberated on the door. Sloane jumped, her tea jostling dangerously close to the edge of the cup and stared at the door.

Robby knew to leave her alone when she was down here. The other employees didn't even know this space was hers. Most assumed it held storage. Or maybe a second office for Sloane. She set her mug down and raced to the door, worried something had gone wrong tonight. Worried, she realized, about Blake.

She opened the door just as another knock came. And there, with rain water dripping down her neck, was Blake.

"Blake, what are you doing here? Are you okay?"

"I don't want you to disappear on me again."

She tried to pull her inside, but Blake stood firm. The rain picked up. But Blake didn't seem to notice. Her eyes flared wide as rain began to fall harder. Her curls were plastered to her neck and she was holding a blanket to her chest.

"I don't know what you're talking about. I'm right here."

"I know I said I needed space to write today. And I did. But I think I told you to stay away because I am scared. But I am also scared you're going to disappear on me again."

"Blake, I'm sorry. I—"

"You have your whole life up here. You have this place, and your friends and your plans. I've spent ten years wondering what happened to you and you've just been up here playing hotel."

"You don't know *anything* I've been through. I—"

"You're right. I don't. Because you never told me. It hasn't been easy for me, okay? I've been in the dark for ten years. When you disappeared, it wrecked me." She shivered and Sloane tracked a rain drop as it ran down her neck and soaked into her collar.

Blake shook her head and seemed to register for the first time that she was dripping wet. "Look, I didn't mean to barge in on you like this. I just need to say that I need more from you. Or…nothing at all."

Blake turned to leave and something snapped inside Sloane. Anger and heat and frustration all at once. That must have been why she reached out, grabbed Blake's wrist and tugged.

"Wait," she choked out.

Blake's pulse hammered beneath Sloane's fingertips. Her gaze met Sloane's with fire and heat and hurt. Sloane wanted to take it away. Even if just for a moment.

“What do you want from me Sloane?” Her chest heaved and her eyes flitted to the point where Sloane was still holding on.

“I don’t know—I can’t think. I just don’t want you to leave,” Sloane ground out. She shouldn’t be doing this. “At least stay here until it stops raining.”

“You can’t just demand things. You can’t take and take but never give—” Blake began. But then she stopped. Sloane must have looked wrecked because Blake took a step closer, her hand falling from Sloane’s grasp.

“What do you *want*, Sloane?” she asked again. Her voice was rough with a hint of frustration. Or was it desperation?

All Sloane knew was that she was tired. She was tired of being strong. Tired of fighting the entire world. Tired of denying that she wished she could do it all again differently.

“Ten years ago…my uncle died.” Sloane huffed out the words she still hated to say. “He was in a car accident. It all happened so fast. And I had to get back here. He put me in charge of this. Of everything. I didn’t have a choice.” Sloane felt her throat tighten as she fought back tears. “So, I’ve been here. And I was a coward. And I should have called—”

Blake reached out a hand and smoothed away

the tears on Sloane's cheeks. When had she started crying?

"I should have called." Her voice was hollow. She couldn't look Blake in the eyes. Blake was right. About all of this. Sloane didn't know what she wanted.

"Hey, it's okay." Blake's voice was a whisper. "I'm sorry. I didn't mean to make you cry. Here, I'll come inside, okay? I'll come in."

CHAPTER ELEVEN

Blake

BLAKE WENT INSIDE. She was tired, and cold, and the rush of sugar was crashing out of her system. All she really wanted to do was collapse into Sloane's arms, but Sloane needed her now. Even if she didn't know how to ask for it.

Sloane's uncles death wasn't a surprise, but seeing the burden it had placed on Sloane definitely was surprising. She seemed hollowed out. A shell of the woman she'd been before.

"I can't talk about it—all of it—right now. It's too much. My uncle, my parents, my cousin." Sloane's breath came out with a hiccup and Blake shook her head. She didn't need Sloane to tell her everything *tonight*. She just needed to know Sloane wasn't going to run away.

For now.

Blake knew that days from now, when she was back home, she might regret this. When she was sitting at her desk, or walking along the booths at a farmer's market, or lying in her bed alone at night, she'd remember this exact moment.

She held Sloane in her arms, pressing kisses to the top of her head. "Thank you for telling me," she murmured. And "I'm here to listen." And "Oh no, I'm getting you all wet."

Sloane let out a small laugh at the last one before catching Blake's gaze. Sloane's eyes burned with a stubborn intensity; a fire ignited by some kind of decision. "I don't care about that. I'm just glad you're here."

"I'm pretty sure I have a puddle beneath me," Blake said with a little shiver. She was certain that she had smudged makeup at her eyes' edges, and that her sheer, wet top hinted at a lace bra underneath.

And Sloane had noticed it, too. Sloane's eyes, glassy and unfocused, met hers; Sloane's neck bobbed as she swallowed hard. A wave of warmth and delicious anticipation spread across her as she recognized her own desire mirrored in Sloane's eyes.

Sloane led her to the small sofa. The rain steadily pattered on the roof, but the cottage was quiet. They sat together, not talking, just taking in the moment. Blake rubbed Sloane's shoulders and murmured soothing words in a hushed voice. Soon the quiet turned into something more, something charged and undeniable. Blake shivered as chills ran down her spine.

They were alone, pressed together, practically clinging to one another. And Blake had never felt so vulnerable, and so certain she needed more.

"You're soaked. You must be freezing. Come here." The burn Sloane's fingertips left in their wake as they pressed into Blake's hips sent her reeling. Heat pooled in her stomach when Sloane's hot breath ghosted along the shell of her ear.

But even knowing how much this might hurt next week, Blake didn't stop. She just needed more. She needed the sharp dig of Sloane's fingernails across her shoulders. She needed more of Sloane's moans. She needed time to stop, and she needed to feel alive again.

"Sloane, I..." Blake needed to tell her. That it had been a long time. That maybe she'd forgotten how to do this. That even though she was hurting and maybe a little bit angry, she still wanted this.

"Shh," Sloane whispered along Blake's neck. A request. A demand. Maybe she needed this just as much as Blake.

"I just need to know you want this. That you want me."

Sloane ran her nose along Blake's throat. "There isn't a single part of me that doesn't want this, Miller. But say the word and I'll stop." She trailed the words like kisses up her neck, along her ear, into her hair. "Tell me to stop."

"Don't. Don't stop." The words tumbled from her mouth in a sigh. Sloane growled in agreement.

Blake decided to stop thinking. Later, she would catalog the quaint space they were in. The mug of tea still steaming on the edge of Sloane's desk. An old patchwork quilt folded across the top of a small sofa. The crystal hanging in the window that would no doubt throw a thousand rainbows across the room tomorrow morning when rain wasn't pelting against the window.

For now, she concentrated on the pressure of Sloane's mouth against hers. Blake cupped Sloane's face, wanting her to know she was in this. She was here. She bit down gently on Sloane's bottom lip, sucking it into her mouth and running her tongue along the edge. She felt Sloane loosen her grip, just a bit, and slump into Blake.

She remembered all the ways she could undo Sloane. Sloane liked to be in charge, but if Blake pressed just right, demanded just enough, Sloane would surrender. And she was surrendering now. "Take me to your bed," Blake demanded.

Sloane grabbed her hand and practically teleported to a small bed on the other side of the room. Blake wanted to laugh, but it made sense. All this luxury surrounded them, but Sloane had a hand-me-down handmade quilt and a single pillow. It was just so Sloane.

"I've missed this," Sloane said as she kissed along Blake's shoulder. "I've been thinking about you all day. I wanted to kiss you this morning. I didn't want to stop. I never want to stop with you."

"You can have me," Blake responded. She was pretending. She just wanted to be as close to Sloane as possible. For as long as possible. "Take it all."

Blake realized, for all the kissing they'd done, they were both still fully clothed. Blake in a long, rain-soaked skirt and cropped tank top, her hair spilling down around her. Sloane in a sleek pair of black joggers and a tank top she no doubt wore under her work shirts. It was tight, threadbare black, and she was braless, her nipples straining against the fabric.

She pushed Sloane down on the edge of the bed and Sloane sat quickly—willing and obedient. Blake thrilled at the idea that with one look she could demand anything she wanted from this woman. It made her feel powerful and also delicate, like she was being given a precious gift. She got to see Sloane like this, when no one else did.

Sloane's hand immediately ran up Blake's

inner thigh, coasting higher and higher. Damn her for wearing a skirt. It made it all too easy to widen her stance, suddenly hungry for Sloane's fingers to move higher and higher.

"Can I touch you?" Sloane begged. She pressed her face into Blake's soft stomach and kissed absently. Blake loved how desperate Sloane was. Those words, along with the way her fingers teased at the soft cotton of her underwear, made Blake want to say yes.

Sloane was more confident now than before. She made relentless eye contact with Blake when she spoke. It was unnerving and wonderful. Sloane looked at her like there was no one else in the world. Like she'd been waiting ten years to ask these questions. As if she didn't already know the answer.

Blake knew how much she wanted Sloane. She knew she'd say yes to anything Sloane asked. That her heart was right there for the taking, and that terrified her. Sloane could have it all. Blake knew it. She wanted Sloane to find out, too. "I need to feel you, Miller. Please?"

It was that word, that please, that made Blake break. There was no control when it came to Sloane. She would give her anything she wanted. She nodded helplessly, already pressing her body closer, giving Sloane the access she wanted.

"I want you," Blake panted into her mouth. "Touch me. See what you do to me."

Sloane

Sloane blocked out everything else in her life and focused on Blake's exposed stomach. Her soft curves had been driving her wild for the past few days. Well, the past decade, if she was being honest. And now that Sloane had successfully stripped Blake down to almost nothing, she noticed a smattering of freckles just above her right hip, the stretch of time across her belly and the goose bumps that ran up her thigh when she used her hands to spread her legs wider.

Blake was different, and also exactly the same. She brushed her fingers along the edge of her hip and bit back a smile. She felt the same, soft and responsive and inviting. Even with all the changes, she was still Blake.

Sloane had changed, too. In all the ways Blake had softened, Sloane had become harder. Her lean muscles were taught from hours of riding and gardening. Her legs sturdy from walking the vineyards. Her skin had a constant sun-kissed bronzing from hours outside. She wondered if Blake noticed, if she cared.

"Let me," she whispered. "Missed you." With a whimper Blake leaned down and covered Sloane's mouth with hers. Blake tasted like cabernet and the wild rain that still clung to parts of her skin. Like all the picnics they hadn't had yet. When Sloane delicately pulled Blake's underwear to the side and ghosted against Blake's skin, she gasped into her mouth.

"Please, Sloane. Please."

Sloane murmured her pleasure at Blake's request and pressed into her warmth. Blake wrapped her arms tighter around Sloane's shoulders and slumped into her a bit more. Sloane loved the feel of Blake's body giving itself over to her. She moved her mouth and her hands to all the places she knew would work for Blake before pulling back at the last minute.

Over and over again. She didn't want this to end. She didn't want to give either of them what they desperately craved too quickly. Because then this would be over. And Sloane needed Blake's body against hers for as long as possible. All night if she could.

Blake whined against Sloane's mouth in frustration. Blake must have realized what she was doing because she ground her body down into Sloane's lap, coaxing Sloane's hand to move toward her center. Sloane chuckled at Blake's not-so-subtle attempt to guide her to right where Blake wanted it most.

Yes, Sloane knew exactly what Blake was

doing. Blake didn't like to be teased; Sloane remembered that well. But Sloane absolutely *lived* for teasing Blake. And she was going to have to deal with it. Just this once.

"How do you remember me so well? How do you remember just what to do?"

"I told you," Sloane said, her voice barely a rasp. "I remember everything about you, sweetheart. Every freckle, every moan, every word you've ever written."

They stayed together like that for a while. Blake seeking more, more, more. Blake bit down on her lip and closed her eyes and then proceeded to explore Sloane's body. Her neck, the curve of her shoulder, the small space between her two breasts.

"Please, I need it," she whimpered. And Sloane would give it to her. Eventually. She'd give her anything she wanted.

When Blake got close to the edge, her moves becoming more frantic, her body seeking the pressure she so desperately desired, Sloane withdrew. She smirked up at Blake.

"Why did you stop?" Blake groaned. Her eyes were bleary and her body was still moving and she looked so gorgeous when she was pouting.

"Because," Sloane said. She stood and wrapped Blake in her arms, turning her so she was against the edge of the bed. She slowly sat her down and laid her back. "I want you like this when you come apart. I want to taste you."

Every one of Sloane's dreams for the last ten years couldn't compare to this moment. She was worried she'd built it up in her head. That she'd turned Blake into some kind of dream girl that reality couldn't compare to. But Blake in her bed, under her hands, was better than her memories. Blake was here. And she was real. And time had only made her softer, more tender and rougher all at once.

Blake ran her hands through Sloane's hair and talked her through what she wanted. For someone who claimed she wasn't pursuing her dreams, she knew exactly what to tell Sloane to do. Sloane pressed kisses up her stomach, up the curve of Blake's neck, and finally sealed her mouth over Blake's.

"I've missed you—I've missed us." Sloane's admission flew out before she could stop it. Sloane felt the lump forming in the back of her throat. Blake looked up at her, her eyes a bleary mess after bliss and maybe a little exhausted.

"Come here," she whispered with a gentle tug. She pulled Sloane down. And then Blake took her time. She touched every part of Sloane as if she were made of glass. As if she might disappear. No one had touched Sloane with this level of care in so, so long.

Blake looked at her like she might disappear. "I'm not going anywhere," Sloane whispered into Blake's hair. She wasn't sure what she meant by those words, but she needed Blake to know. She wasn't going to run. She wasn't going to disappear.

"Shh," Blake whispered. "Later." And then Sloane didn't think anymore. All she could register was the gentleness of Blake's touch, the softness of her lips, and the profound sense of forgiveness and understanding in their embrace.

And then she was close and then she was gone. Shattered into a thousand pieces and glad about it. Her eyes stung and she swore she wouldn't cry. Blake covered her in more kisses and pulled the quilt up around both of them.

Sloane's eyes kept drifting shut. Blake curled into her arms, soft and warm. It made Sloane feel soft and warm, too. Pieces of her coming back to life that hadn't been pliable in over ten years. There was something about Blake Miller that made Sloane *want* to be soft.

Maybe that's why she had run away? She could have called Blake. She'd stared at her contact in her phone so many times. But she had turned to stone ten years ago. It was what her cousin needed. It was what her parents had demanded. If she let one crack show, they would have swooped in and demanded access to Nico. To the money. To everything.

If she had reached out to Blake, she wouldn't have been able to make it through. But maybe now she could melt, just a little. She could find a small part of her to be vulnerable. And let Blake see all of her.

Sloane fell asleep with her face pressed into Blake's hair, her mouth whispering unintelligible promises as Blake slept. Promises she hoped she could keep.

CHAPTER TWELVE

Blake

THE WALK BACK to the honeymoon suite was lit with the last moments of silver moonlight as the crickets serenaded Blake with their chirps. *Tell us everything*, they seemed to sing. But Blake just pulled the quilt closer as she continued up the path, past the main resort, and to her cottage.

She hadn't meant to fall asleep in Sloane's arms, but the bed had been so warm, and her body had been so thoroughly wrung out and the rain had lulled her into a deep sleep.

She woke in the last few moments when bottomless night transitioned to deep gray morning—maybe her body was still on hot-air balloon time—and inspiration had struck. She'd wrapped the blanket close and slipped away.

In the edges of gray dawn, Blake sat down at the table on her secluded porch and wrote. She captured the day, weaving moments into a tapestry, a history, a patchwork quilt of their memories stitched together like the orchards and vineyards from a thousand feet in the air. More words that would go nowhere. But still, writing them down made the moment seem more real.

She'd nodded off in her chair, the quilt around her shoulders, her eyes heavy and her hand no longer able to hold her pen.

When she woke, she was freezing, the furniture coated in morning dew and the entire world smelling alive, awash in the rain from the night before. Her body was sore in the most delicious way and she stretched out like a cat, searching for a patch of sunlight.

A soft knock announced her daily breakfast delivery, which was already waiting on the doormat of her front door. This was the kind of pampering that felt like too much. Like they knew her too well. A tray laden with an array of fruits, local honey and warm scones. There were fresh flowers arranged in a whimsical pattern. Wildflowers burst out of the jar haphazardly. Blake snapped a few photos on her phone to save them for a post later. She took the tray to her small table on the porch and drizzled honey over a scone.

I could get used to this. She knew that this wasn't what being a writer was like all the time. She knew one-week stays in luxury resorts wasn't the norm, but still. There was no shortage of things to write about. Or photos to take. Or reasons to swoon. Not that she would be writing about Sloane in her article.

Her article. She needed to buckle down and write some more words for Tara. She stared at her journal, bursting with all the things she couldn't say. All the things she couldn't put in a travel review.

Her phone chirped on the nightstand and she reluctantly left the morning tableau to see who it was. It could be Sloane. It could be her mom, trying to confirm plans for her end of summer visit. When Blake had come home that summer, she'd been too sad to visit her parents. But her mother must have known something was wrong. She'd shown up a week later with a carry-on full of face masks and romance novels.

She didn't ask any questions. She just sat next to Blake, side by side. She'd planned a girls' trip like that one every summer since. Blake always looked forward to them.

But it wasn't her mom. It was her boss. All the warm, fuzzy feelings Blake had stirred up vanished in an instant. The message read, Call me asap. She also had missed two calls. She must have read the notes.

Blake took a deep breath and messaged back, Ready when you are.

A video call immediately came through. *Crap.* Blake was not expecting a FaceTime from her boss at nine o'clock the morning after, well, after last night. But she couldn't back out now. She sat down on the patio and pressed the green answer button.

"Tara. Good morning—"

"Blake, I'm going to get right down to it."

This wasn't shocking. Tara always *got right down to it*. It was a signature phrase other people used in the office when impersonating her. Maybe Tara was going to give her more inches for the article. Maybe she wanted to make it a segment. Maybe Blake had impressed her so much she was going to give her her next assignment now.

"I'm going to need you to start from scratch."

"I'm sorry?"

"We can't use any of this. We're a travel magazine. Our readers want to know about the location, they want to feel like they're there. They don't want…this."

Blake's head spun with confusion. "Tara, I'm not sure what you mean. My notes *are* about the location. The options. What this place has in store. I thought the writing was okay?"

"Yes, Blake, the writing is fine. But this article needs more than fine. There's no heart here. It's like reading your grocery list. Or an edit list. Or—" Tara snapped her fingers and Blake flinched. "That's it. You're writing this like you're written a caption. I need you to write it with heart."

Blake felt her own heart in her throat. She couldn't write a story with heart and not tell the whole truth. Her feelings for Sloane would be apparent. She wouldn't be impartial. A story with heart…meant a story she couldn't tell. "With heart? I'm a journalist, Tara—"

"You're also someone who told me to take a chance. You told me you could do this. Are you telling me you *can't* do this? Because I can pull this. I can bring you back. If it's too much, tell me now."

Blake's stomach flipped. She couldn't give up on this. Not now. "I can do this, Tara. I have more notes. I have more…ideas. Give me a few more days."

Tara's lips pursed on the other end of the line. "You have two days. If I don't have something workable in my inbox in forty-eight hours, I'm pulling this. I gave you this chance because I saw something in you. Don't make me regret this. Vella West was a big enough name to pull in our advertising quota for the quarter."

"Okay, just send me my notes and I'll get going."

"Blake. There are no notes. My note is *start over*. Give me something I can leave notes on. Understood?"

Blake swallowed and willed her eyes not to water. “Understood.”

“Good.” Blake could feel Tara’s stare through the phone. She was scrutinizing her the way she’d scour over layouts and spreadsheets. “And for goodness’ sake, do something with your hair. You look like you were rolling around all night. I hope this isn’t how you’re traipsing around a five-star resort. You’re an ambassador of our brand when you’re there, Blake. Don’t forget that.”

And with that, the call ended. Blake slumped back in the chair and let out a shaky sigh. This was bad. This was really bad. Blake needed a plan. She would take a shower, make a list and head down to the lobby to see what else she could scope out.

Blake had been so careful to keep her emotions out of her writing. Because if she didn’t, she knew anyone could see how her feelings for Sloane were all over everything she’d ever done. Why did Sloane have to work for this hotel? Why did she have to be here?

This wasn’t doing her any good. Sloane *was* here. She *did* work for this hotel. And she wasn’t going anywhere. Blake didn’t *want* her to go anywhere.

Well, that was a sobering thought. Blake needed caffeine. She needed a reset. She would shower, review her notes, and then find Robby.

Maybe they could tell her about some of these local products—she could include it in her write up. That would be sure to add some heart. She uploaded photos of the resort and got to work.

A few hours later as she entered the lobby, her phone pinged with a message from an unknown number. She opened it wearily.

I hope you don't mind, but your number was in your file.

I had a really good time last night. Unexpected. But good.

This is Sloane by the way.

Blake's stomach flipped.

I have meetings all day, but I'd love to join you on the train tonight. There are some things I want to tell you. I know I waited too long, but I think it's time we talked.

Blake didn't respond right away, but her heart surged with hope. The wine train had been included in the itinerary, but Blake had been too nervous to ask Sloane if she planned to attend what was essentially a Very Romantic Date.

Excited butterflies flittered through her as if she was the lavender outside. Sloane was finally keeping her promises.

Sloane

The pile of papers on Sloane's desk was so high it was leaning like a wobbly Jenga tower. Robby was going to kill her if she didn't get things under control, and fast. There were multiple requests for interviews, two vendors hoping to have their wine stocked in the restaurants and more than one reporter sniffing around. Sloane didn't do interviews. She didn't do public. If she could be a silent investor in this hotel, she would.

She just wanted to make it magical. And not get any of the credit. Her phone buzzed and she lunged for it. She'd texted Blake hours ago and still hadn't heard back from her. She was practically vibrating from nerves and caffeine. She'd felt a bit sweaty and a bit unnerved when she woke to an empty bed. Her sheets still smelled like lavender and rose. Being surrounded by Blake's smell was sweet, sweet torture.

Sounds great. She had responded. A new nervous wound around Sloane's chest.

"Why are you staring at your screen?" Robby's voice brought her back into the moment. She closed her messages and tossed her phone on her desk. They weren't going to get anything out of her.

"Come to think of it, you were smiling when you walked in earlier. This wouldn't have anything to do with the gorgeous woman staying in the honeymoon suite, would it?"

"Of course not," Sloane said, not meeting Robby's eyes. She felt them glare at her as she sorted the papers. "Just a good day, I suppose. Everything is on track."

Robby snorted and sat in the chair across from Blake with their legs crossed and a knowing scowl. "Boss, we've got a problem."

"Oh?" Sloane began staking papers into neat piles, ignoring the way Robby's glare was penetrating to her soul, as if they somehow knew what she'd been up to the night before.

"Yes. Someone sent room service to Blake's room this morning. And apparently there was an arrangement of flowers."

Sloane's shuffling paused for just a moment before she continued making haphazard piles. Of course, Robby knew about the breakfasts. Robby knew everything. "Well, that's thoughtful."

"It would be—if the hotel had done it." Robby took the last sip of their coffee before setting it down gently on the edge of the desk. "It's not part of the package. It's not in the agreement."

Sloane felt her body flush. She had just wanted to do something nice. Blake loved fresh flowers. Sloane could still remember the way Blake would daisy-chain together what were basically weeds, turning them into bracelets or flower crowns for the two of them in Italy. She'd spend hours weaving them into the perfect jewelry. Sloane felt cherished whenever Blake put a bright green stem around her finger or tucked a flower behind her ear.

She hadn't meant to become this secret deliverer of pastries and peonies. She'd snuck into the resort's garden and gathered some blooms together the best she knew how before sneaking into the kitchen and swiping some scones and local honey. And she'd been doing it all week.

"It's not a big deal. Just a simple breakfast. And, honestly, a really terrible floral arrangement."

"Terrible?" Robby raised a brow. "Now, I *know* it was you."

"I admit nothing."

"Well, I hope it *wasn't* you. Because then it could be seen as bribing a reviewer. You took her in your hot-air balloon. You ignored the group protocol. And now you're sending flowers. This could ruin us. If it goes sideways—"

"It's not going to go sideways."

"How do you know that?"

"Because, I—" Sloane opened and closed her mouth several times. "There's no way Blake would do that. Blake would know none of this was a bribe simply for a good review."

Robby smiled sadly at her. "Oh, babe. I really hope you're right."

"Right about what?" A cheerful voice called from behind Sloane.

Sloane's stomach fell to the ground. What was Nico doing here? He swept into the room with the air of an emcee, dropping his leather overnight bag into the chair and pulling off his sunglasses.

"Nico?" Robby raised an eyebrow and gave Sloane a look. "I didn't know you were coming."

Her cousin shouldn't be here. He should be in school. He should be studying. "What are you doing here?"

He scooped Sloane into a hug and pulled her close. He kissed the top of her head before lifting her in his arms and squeezing tight. She still remembered the day he realized he was taller than her. During his sophomore year, a sudden growth spurt brought him to six feet tall. It had him whooping with glee in the kitchen, teasing Sloane about how he could reach something on the top shelf for her. He was such a dork.

"I think what you meant to say was, baby cousin, I missed you. I'm so glad you're here for my big weekend."

She laughed as she held him at arm's length and took him in. He looked tired, but his eyes seemed focused and he seemed okay. "Yes, that, too. But I thought I told you to stay back and study."

"Pffft. And miss this? No way." He stared

down at her desk and frowned. "Besides, I knew something was wrong when I called." He tugged on the front of her bob and tucked it behind her ear.

Dammit. Sloane, when stressed, had a habit of tucking and retucking her hair. He must have seen her nervous tic and now he was here, missing classes, just to check on her.

Nico studied her face, searching for answers. "Okay, that's it." He tugged on her hand. "We need to get you out of here. Why are you stuck at your desk? It's your big week."

Sloane was not going to tell her cousin that she'd actually spent the last forty-eight hours flirting and kissing and, well…she wasn't going to tell him any of that.

"Come on. I want to see my horse. I want to get some fresh air. Robby, you coming?"

"No. I have a lot to do. You two catch up." Robby waved them off as they took over Sloane's job of organizing papers. "Sloane, please don't forget about what I said."

Sloane swallowed thickly. Robby was right. She was putting everything at risk each moment she spent with Blake. But she just wasn't sure if she was going to be able to stop.

CHAPTER THIRTEEN

Blake

WHEN BLAKE ARRIVED in the lobby for the wine train, Robby greeted her with a town car. Worry crept up the back of her neck. If Robby had called for a car, then Sloane wasn't coming.

"Right this way, Ms. Miller."

Blake crooked her head at them. She didn't want to ask and risk disappointment flashing clear across her face.

"Don't worry. Ms. Vella is planning on joining you," Robby offered anyway. "She had some business to attend to and will meet you at the train."

Blake nodded and forced a smile. "Thank you, Robby. I appreciate it." She kept her tone light and didn't let her face drop until after she was tucked into the car. This is what she had been worried about. Sloane was a very busy person. Her life was full of obligations and commitments. And those things were more important than Blake.

When she arrived, a vintage train, completely renovated, waited on the tracks. Each car glimmered in the evening light, reminiscent of the old trains she'd seen in museums with formal dining cars and luxurious textiles.

Once inside, Blake realized she was in a private car. There was a couch, an elegant table setting and plenty of space to walk around. The windows were ajar, letting a soft summer breeze trickle through the windows. Everything looked custom selected: antiques in warm woods, brass fixtures and modern amenities. A bottle of wine chilled next to the table in an elaborate silver tub.

Someone cleared their throat from the far end of the car and Blake realized she wasn't alone. Sloane stood and walked toward her. Her hair was down and she wore a soft black camisole with wide white dress pants. She looked softer somehow, and absolutely gorgeous. The business suit was nowhere to be seen.

"Wow, look at you," Blake said in awe. "You look stunning."

A flash of pink crept up Sloane's neck. "Thank you," she murmured. Blake felt Sloane's gaze travel down her and back up again. "And I'm sorry about earlier. I had some family come in unexpectedly."

Blake bit the edge of her lip. Sloane had promised her she was a priority this week. And she wanted to believe her. But her tardiness had awoken worries from the past. "Family?"

"My cousin, Nico. He showed up unexpectedly and we spent some time catching up. But still, I should have called."

Blake's need to respond was drowned out by the train whistle. An announcer's voice came over the loudspeaker of the train. Blake wasn't even sure where the speakers were hiding. "We'll be leaving in just a moment. Please make sure you're seated and ready to enjoy the rambling vineyard hills, the incredible view and the romantic setting. Welcome to Napa."

Sloane gestured to the leather chesterfield sofa and the two women sat down. The train creaked and rumbled before starting on its path.

"This all feels so surreal," Blake admitted. "You, this train, this view."

Sloane poured her wine and passed her the glass.

"Tell me about your writing. I want to know more."

Blake knew she needed to be honest with Sloane. She just wasn't sure where to start. Or how much to share. "I'm not a writer. I mean, not anymore. Or maybe not yet? I've worked as social media manager for the last ten years. And

I'm good at it. So, every time the opportunity arose to write, I didn't apply, didn't pitch my ideas. I love parts of my job. My colleagues are the best. But it always felt like there was part of me I was closing off. After you left—"

"Blake, I—"

"No, it's okay. You don't owe me anything. I did this to myself. After you left, I felt lost. I felt like I didn't deserve my dreams. So, I didn't pursue them. But seeing you this week, seeing what you've accomplished. It makes me realize my dreams are worth pursuing."

Sloane smiled sadly at Blake and shook her head. "Your dreams *are* worth pursuing. And I love my work now. I love my cousin. I can't regret how things turned out. But I wasn't pursuing a dream. I was cleaning up someone else's. When my uncle died, I had to hit Pause on everything of mine. It took years to untangle his finances. I was working my own job, managing his estate, and I became Nico's guardian. It was…a lot for me."

"Sloane, I didn't know." Suddenly, her cousin's arrival made a lot more sense. Sloane was practically a parent. Of course, she'd make time for her cousin. Blake tried to remember what she'd been like at twenty-two. There's no way she would have been ready to take on being a full-time parent on top of everything else Sloane had. The weight of it would have been too much for her.

But Sloane had managed it. Somehow.

"I know. I didn't tell you. I didn't tell *anyone*. I didn't want anyone to think I wasn't capable. Especially not my cousin. I'm all he has left. My parents were awful about it. They didn't understand why they didn't get custody of my cousin and oversight of the estate."

"I mean, that was a lot to put on you at twenty-two."

Sloane shrugged. "Maybe. But no one expected my uncle to go so soon." She took another sip of wine and pursed her lips together. "But we did okay. Nico and I. We figured it out together. And now he's in college. He's almost done. And I was able to open the resort."

"It is pretty amazing." Blake lifted her eyes to meet Sloane's. There were soft lines at the edges Blake hadn't noticed before. No doubt from years of trying to be everything to everyone. "*You're* pretty amazing. I can't believe you did all that."

"I'm so glad you like it. I have you to thank for all the details."

"What do you mean?"

Sloane fell quiet, her fingers twisting gently in her lap as if the truth had to be coaxed out of her.

"Every time I had to make a decision," she

said softly, "I thought of you—of that summer. I'd ask myself, '*What would Blake love?*' The light in the room, the linens on the bed, even the shampoo. I think, without even realizing it, I was trying to bring it all back. Like if I could just re-create it, piece by piece…maybe you'd come back. Maybe your heart would recognize it and find its way to me."

She looked up then, her eyes full and open, golden sunset catching the tears she hadn't let fall.

"And you did."

The words settled into Blake like a warm breeze through tall grass—soft and unexpected, stirring something she'd long tucked away. She had dreamed of this moment for so long that the idea of it had become abstract. But this was real. Sloane was here, speaking the kind of truth that tasted like late summer and first love.

And still—her heart fluttered with nerves, with disbelief, with fear.

It was so much to take in. So much to hold. This woman, this moment—it was everything she'd wanted. And yet, it made her feel fragile in the most exquisite way, like something delicate and treasured that might break from too much feeling.

She leaned in, closing the space between them with a kiss as soft as evening light on wine-dark lips. It was gentle, careful, full of memory and longing. She could taste the berries and the currants—the same ones they'd picked that first week—bittersweet and lush, alive with possibility.

"You didn't have to re-create the past," Blake whispered, her voice barely louder than the breeze. "You just had to pick up the phone."

"I know," Sloane breathed, her voice catching. "I know. I just didn't know how to say I was sorry. Or how to ask for another chance. I never really believed you'd show up."

Sloane

Sloane hadn't planned on telling Blake any of this—at least not in this order. She planned to start with: *My cousin is here.* And then, *by the way I was his guardian.* And then, *I sort of still am.* But Blake's floral dress wrapped around her body in the same way so many dresses had that summer. When they'd hopped a train and traveled from one side of Europe to the other. When they'd woken up in Rome and decided that they needed to leave for the coast immediately. Both of them giggling and shoving clothes into each other's suitcases, kissing and laughing and free.

Blake still had wild soft curls, a wide smile and eyes the color of the sea. Sitting with her tonight was like revisiting a dream. But better.

Because Blake had a scar on her finger and a few silver threads in her hair and Sloane knew she was really here. This wasn't a dream.

A server brought them dinner covered in silver trays. They moved to a small rectangular table along the windows, draped in velvet and fine china. They spent time focusing on the now. Sloane told her about Rhett and Winnie. How stubborn he had been. And how he insisted on staying.

Blake's eyes sparkled with mirth as she teased Sloane about having so much in common with her horse. The conversation flowed as easily as the wine, and Sloane couldn't imagine a better way to spend a night. It was nothing like their stilted dinner less than a week ago the night Blake arrived.

"I like you like this," Blake said, hiding a smile behind her lips. "You're more confident now."

"It's Robby." Sloane sighed. "They won't let me get away with anything less."

"Well, good for them." Blake laughed with abandon and took a bite of dinner. "So, what's next for you, Sloane?"

Sloane felt nerves tense in her stomach. She didn't want to think about what came next. She knew what her uncle would have wanted. Expansion. She knew Robby and Nico were both depending on her to do whatever it took to ensure Vella West stayed profitable and secure.

And she knew, deep down, that all she wanted was a quiet cottage, a cup of tea and someone to share it with.

She shook her head. "Nope. No work talk tonight." She dropped her napkin onto the edge of the table and stood, holding out her hand. "Come with me?"

Blake blinked at her before dropping her own napkin and taking her hand. "Where? We are on a train."

"Trust me."

She opened the door at the end of the car and the rush of air swept into the room. They weren't going fast; it was barely a ramble as they slowly passed by hills and groves of trees. They stepped into the neighboring car, which wasn't really a car at all.

When Sloane invested in the wine train, she'd insisted on creating this space. A private dining car with an adjoining courtyard of sorts. It was an open-air train car with live plants and strung lights and three-hundred-sixty-degree views of their surroundings. Soft music played around them, a slow, gorgeous Italian love song.

The music couldn't muffle Blake's intake of breath. "Sloane—I—this song." Sloane stepped closed and offered her hand. Blake took it and Sloane pulled her close.

"Dancing with you outside the Cafe de Sol

was one of my best memories. Dance with me, again?"

Blake nodded, teary-eyed, and fell into Sloane's embrace. Sloane was just enough taller than Blake that her head rested perfectly in the crook of her neck. They swayed back and forth as the song played all around them.

The air was full of earth and vine and the edge of summer. The moment just before the harvest. Sloane knew that smell well. She inhaled deeply, also getting hints of Blake's shampoo and body-wash. Her heart clenched, knowing this was the moment she would remember most when this was over.

When Blake was gone, when she inevitably left for home, when her article went viral. Sure, she was in Sloane's arms now. But there was no promise of tomorrow. And Sloane couldn't even ask for it. She was the one who'd left ten years ago. She didn't get to request more. That had to come from Blake.

She just needed to make Blake want to ask. She pressed a gentle kiss into Blake's hair and felt her own eyes prick with tears when Blake squeezed her hand.

"This is so magical. Do all your guests get this special treatment?" Blake teased.

"No one else has ever seen this space," Sloane confided. "I had it remodeled about a year ago.

Sometimes I take the train and just sit here. But no one else."

"Why not? It's beautiful. You could make it part of the resort. You could—"

Sloane shook their head. "Sometimes it's nice to have something just for you."

As if on cue, a faint buzzing filled the space. Blake pulled away, confused. Sloane tried to ignore it, but her phone buzzed again from her hip. She fished the phone out of her pocket and saw the obvious hurt on Blake's face.

Robby.

Why was Robby calling?

Sloane silenced the call and held it in front of her. "I'm so sorry," she murmured. "It's Robby."

"You can answer it." Blake backed away more, heading to the bench at the edge of the courtyard train car. She *should* answer it. Something could be wrong.

"Robby, unless this is an absolute emergency, I have full faith in you and Nico to take care of things until I'm done with this date."

The phone was silent for a moment and then Robby's voice said quickly, "You got it, boss."

Sloane swiped the screen and turned her phone off before pocketing it again.

"What are you doing?" Blake said. "It could be important. What if something happened?"

Sloane strode over to Blake and wrapped her in her arms, she crowded her against the wall.

"Robby is very capable. They can handle anything for two hours. I want to be here with you."

"Are you sure?"

No, she wasn't sure everything would be okay. But it would get fixed if it wasn't. Besides, she was in the middle of a train ride. It wasn't as if she could stop the train and helicopter back to the resort. Well, to be fair, she probably could but she wasn't going to.

She was here, with Blake in her arms. And she intended to make the most of it.

"I'm sure. I'd like to introduce you to Nico tomorrow. If that's okay with you? But for now, there's nowhere else I need to be than here with you." She ran her nose along Blake's jaw and pressed a kiss just behind her ear. "Please Blake, can I kiss you?"

"You don't have to ask, Sloane. This mouth is yours. Do whatever you want."

Sloane raised one brow and kissed her. Slow. She drank her in. "We have about ten minutes before they show up with dessert."

"There's a lot we could do in ten minutes."

Sloane kissed her again; a smirk played at the corner of her lips. "Yes, I intend to find out."

CHAPTER FOURTEEN

Blake

BLAKE NEEDED A dose of reality. For days, she'd been swept up in a world of curated luxury—meals comped, spa treatments like dreams and views so flawless they looked staged. And Sloane. Sloane's lingering looks, gentle touches and constant presence in Blake's thoughts had been a welcome distraction.

She had to get off the resort. Everything around her was a carefully curated moment—the view from her balcony, the pastries at breakfast, even the plush terry cloth robe hanging in her bathroom. Now that she knew the truth behind Vella West's creation, it felt like the past was everywhere, pressing in from all sides.

Robby arranged for a car to bring her to downtown Napa. Buildings clustered closely together, a mix of classic brick architecture and bright windows. Custom-painted signs and open doors welcomed shoppers. It struck Blake how San

Diego was less than ten hours away, yet it felt like an entirely different world as she walked the streets of Napa.

She turned down Front Street, passing a bistro with soft jazz spilling from hidden speakers and a couple clinking glasses on the patio. The river ran along the street. The slow and steady movement of water brought a sense of calm to her frazzled thoughts.

Sloane had a cousin. She had been his guardian. And she'd raised him for the last ten years. That was why she hadn't called. It was both satisfying and incredibly sad to know that Sloane hadn't meant to disappear. Blake hadn't done anything wrong either. But she'd spent the last ten years dissecting every moment to figure out why Sloane would disappear on her. It didn't make the hurt less, but it helped her understand.

As she wandered, an overhead sign caught her eye—the same insignia that adorned the shampoo and bodywash bottles from the resort's bathrooms. She ducked into the shop; her footsteps soft on the wooden floor. The air was warm and fragrant—lavender, cedar, something citrusy she couldn't quite place. Shelves were lined with soaps wrapped in linen and tiny bottles of custom scents, all catching the late afternoon light and glowing like little hidden treasures.

The shop was soft, inviting, the kind of place

that made her want to curl up with a book and forget the rest of the world.

"Looking for something in particular?"

The woman's voice was soft with a bit of rasp, like a quiet breeze on a lazy afternoon. She stepped out from behind the counter, her round glasses catching the light. Her fingers were adorned with a smattering of silver rings and she waved them around as if each one held a story.

Blake hesitated, then pulled the brown glass jar from her bag and held it out to the woman. "I'm staying at the Vella West. Do you have more of this rose and lavender blend?"

The woman's smile softened, but there was a flicker of something deeper in her eyes as she cradled the jar, turning it slowly.

"That one's special," she said quietly. "Not usually out on the shelves."

Blake raised an eyebrow, curiosity blooming alongside a sudden ache. "Oh?"

The woman glanced up, thoughtful. "It was made custom. A collaboration with the resort."

Blake's breath caught, though she didn't speak. She clutched the tiny bottle to her chest. Perhaps this woman could tell Blake something that would ease her anxious heart. "Do you know the owner well?"

The woman paused, then laughed softly, as if

recalling a secret. "Sloane Vella? I've known her since she was a kid. Came out here every summer, riding horses, running wild in the hills with her uncle, rest his soul."

Blake's fingers tightened around the jar. The girl the woman was describing, that was the Sloane she remembered, too. A bit wild. A bit less controlled than the woman she'd been spending time with this week.

Sloane must have felt so lonely in those first few years. It must have been awful. To be twenty-two, your mentor gone, the weight of the world on your shoulders.

"She seems to have done just fine," Blake said, her voice barely a whisper.

"Well, yes she has," the woman agreed. "Grief has a funny way. It doesn't go away, just grows around you. Do you…know her?"

"I do," Blake said. "I mean, I did. Before."

"Well, in that case…" She looked Blake up and down with consideration before selecting a different jar from a shelf behind her. She placed it into a brown paper bag, folded the top carefully and handed it to Blake. "Take this one," she said softly.

Blake wasn't sure what to say, so she nodded, clutching the bag as she murmured thanks and stepped back into the golden light.

Outside, the sun was dipping low, casting long

shadows across the quiet street. Blake wandered past shuttered bookstores and vibrant art galleries until she found a cafe tucked between two old stone buildings.

She ordered an tea she barely tasted and sat beneath the green canopy, pulling a worn linen-covered notebook from her bag—the one she carried everywhere but rarely opened. Its soft edges reminded her of the journals she'd kept during her younger, braver days, full of uncertain hopes and Sloane's name scribbled in the margins.

Her pen hovered for a long time before she set it down and huffed out an annoyed breath. She could do this. She needed to finish her article. She flexed her fingers. Maybe some lotion would help. When she unscrewed the lid, she was hit with peppermint, rosemary and…tea tree oil. She was hit with Sloane. Sloane up late at night sipping peppermint tea. Sloane, who would spend the mornings picking vibrant herbs, their scent a delicious mix of sweet and savory, but she was clueless about how to transform them into a meal. Blake rubbed a dab of lotion into the back of her hands before taking one more breath.

The scent, the memory, the fragile thread between past and present hit her all at once. Words poured out of her—anger, heartbreak, yearning and a quiet hope she hadn't dared voice. Page after page, her handwriting grew messier, ink smudged where her hand pressed hard. It wasn't a pitch. It wasn't neat. But it was hers. Honest and raw.

Maybe this was what she needed before she could figure out what came next. It hurt to rip open the past and sift through her memories. It hurt to think about returning from Europe, alone and heartbroken. Through blurred vision and a second round of tea, she wrote it all down.

When the sun slipped below the hills, casting the streets in amber and lavender, Blake tucked the notebook away and made her way back toward Vella West. The resort glowed like a storybook scene—warm lights flickering behind ivy-laced windows, the hills bathed in soft twilight.

The lobby was quiet when she arrived, the hush that settles at day's end when guests shower off sun and salt and settle with wine.

Sloane sat behind the desk, a tablet propped in front of her and a half-empty glass of sparkling water close by.

Blake hesitated, then stepped closer.

Sloane looked up and smiled, her eyes widening just a bit as she took in Blake. "How was your trip into town?"

"Good," Blake said, not knowing how to put the afternoon into words. Blake glanced down at the bag, thumb brushing the folded top. "Can I ask you something?"

Sloane spoke with no hesitation. "Anything."

"The flowers on the breakfast trays. The ones with herbs mixed in. Do you know where they come from? A woman at the apothecary gave me this scent and it reminds me of the herbs and flowers I get every day."

Sloane blinked once, like the question caught her off guard, then recovered, straightening a notepad on the desk.

"Well," she said, "some things are meant to stay a little magical for guests, Miss Miller."

"You said I could ask you anything," Blake challenged. There was a story here—not the kind for her article—something deeper. Something distinctly Sloane. She needed to know the answer. "And I want to know."

Sloane sighed and dropped her tablet. The look in her eyes was part defeat and part satisfaction, as if she had been hoping Blake would press the issue.

"Fine. There's a wildflower garden past the olive tree grove at the far perimeter of the property." Sloane leaned in close. "It's not really open to guests, but no one's going to stop you if you wander. Just…be kind to it."

Something settled deep in Blake's chest. This was a clue. A secret. Sloane was letting her in even more. She felt dizzy with the possibility and the promise. She needed to see this place. "Will you take me?"

Sloane

Blake was in her garden.

More than the stables, more than her tiny cottage, these wildflower fields were hers. The place she came when grief was too big to hold in her arms. She would come out here and wander and talk to the flowers. She'd whisper words to them and they never judged.

Sloane stood watching Blake from a distance, heart pounding with the weight of everything left unsaid. The olive trees swayed gently overhead; their twisted trunks bathed in the soft amber of evening light. Their silver leaves rustled like whispers in the wind, as if the earth itself was trying to comfort her. But nothing could settle the storm inside her.

Part of her wanted to walk away. She could leave Blake alone out here and retreat to the safety of her office. Or her house. She could have dinner with Nico. She could balance some books. There were a million things she could be doing.

But she crossed the distance and approached Blake.

"Well, this is it," Sloane said. Blake turned, her fingers brushing the fragrant stems of a lavender bush and smiled at the sight of Sloane. It made Sloane's heart feel too big for her chest.

"This is what?"

"My grieving spot. My…everything spot. This is where I come when I need to… I don't know. When I need to not be anywhere."

Sloane had left for Europe planning to soak in the wisdom of the world. She was going to wade into the waters of viticulture slowly, learning side by side with her uncle when she returned. But the universe had made other plans.

Blake reached out and took Sloane's hand. The simple gesture meant more than words. Sloane squeezed and then let go.

"I know I apologized for not calling you," she murmured to Blake, her voice barely more than a whisper. "But I don't regret it. I need you to understand why I closed myself off. I had to plan my uncle's funeral. Take care of Nico. Everything fell on me. I didn't want to burden anyone else. I'm *glad* I didn't put that on you."

She pulled her arms tightly around herself, as if she was still holding the fractured pieces of her heart together. She had felt broken, scattered, the life she'd built for herself disintegrating with every responsibility that had fallen on her. But Sloane never let anyone see just how shattered she was inside. She'd been strong for Nico, for her uncle's employees, for the land. And it was too much. It was all too much for someone to carry alone.

"You could have—"

"You wouldn't have wanted that," Sloane cut her off, the words slipping from her lips without thinking. "I couldn't ask you to be part of this. I couldn't ask you to help carry this weight with me. This weight I'm *still* carrying with me. Every day. I have hard days. I have days when all I want to do is cry. I can be messy. And mean. You don't want that."

Blake's sharp retort came swiftly. "You don't know that. You never gave me a chance."

Sloane's heart clenched, guilt and regret knotting in her stomach. Blake wasn't just angry—she was hurt. And Sloane had never meant to hurt her. Her responsibilities were hers alone; no one could blame her for not telling a girl she'd been kissing along the coast for two months. That would have been ridiculous.

"We'd only known each other for half a summer," Sloane whispered, the lie tasting bitter on her tongue. It had felt like more, so much more. They had connected in ways Sloane hadn't anticipated, and now that connection was back. And it felt like a life raft in a sea of chaos.

"I don't know how to do this," Sloane confessed, her voice trembling, vulnerable in a way she rarely allowed herself to be. "I'm used to things just being thrust on me. I never wanted to burden anyone. I just—I want to protect you. I thought if you saw all of this—this mess, this chaos—you'd walk away."

A decade of silence stretched between them; Blake stood motionless, the air thick with the scent of old regrets and unspoken words. The silence felt thick enough to suffocate. Finally, Blake's voice cracked through the stillness, quieter than before but sharp with emotion.

"You think I wouldn't have wanted to be a part of all of this?" Blake asked softly, her words falling from her lips like a challenge, raw with the pain Sloane hadn't seen. "You think I wouldn't have wanted to be there with you? I'm not the one who walked away, Sloane."

Sloane's chest tightened, and she stepped forward, not sure if she was seeking Blake's forgiveness or if she just needed her close. The gulf between them felt wide, and Sloane wasn't sure how to bridge it. She reached for Blake's hand, but the distance between them remained. "You shouldn't have had to be part of this," Sloane whispered. "I didn't want to burden you with *my* problems, with Nico, with everything."

Blake took a shaky breath before finally speaking, her voice thick with emotion. "You think I wasn't burdened too?" Her words hit harder than Sloane had expected, and they left a mark. "You think I don't know what it's like to carry everything alone?"

Blake's eyes glistened with unshed tears, and she took a slow, deliberate step toward Sloane, closing the space between them. "I had dreams, you know. I was chasing them with *you*. I was going to write about our adventures. And then you disappeared."

Blake blinked and let out a slow breath. Her next words came out softly, as if she was choosing them carefully. "When I got back to New York, my drive was gone. I didn't want to take on anything that wasn't a guarantee. So, I spent way too many years working as an intern, fetching coffee for the people who were taking risks and doing the writing. It took me ten years to work up the courage to try again. You're not the only one who felt abandoned, Sloane."

Sloane's chest ached at the admission, the rawness of Blake's words cutting through her like a knife. She reached out, trembling, brushing a tear from Blake's cheek, before cupping her face gently. "I never meant to make you feel abandoned. Never."

Blake closed her eyes for a moment, letting the cool air wash over her, as if searching for the right words. When she opened them again, they were filled with something deeper—something Sloane could no longer deny. "You didn't trust me. Not with all of you. How can I trust anything now?"

Sloane took a steadying breath. "I didn't trust *myself*," she confessed. "I didn't think I could handle losing you. I didn't think I could handle—any of this."

Blake's eyes softened, but the vulnerability still lingered in them, raw and unspoken. "But you did. You did this all by yourself," Blake said, her voice barely above a whisper. "And you should be so damn proud of what you've accomplished. We were both so young, and stubborn and selfish. But we aren't those girls anymore. And you can choose. Do you still want to be alone? Or are you ready to let me in?"

"Blake, I—"

"It's okay, take some time." Blake pressed a kiss to Sloane's temple. Even then, Sloane could feel her pulling away. Putting some distance back between them. "I'm not asking you to have all the answers. Why don't we both take some time? I'll see you tomorrow night at the reception."

With a final glance, Blake turned and walked away. Sloane stood frozen in her sanctuary, the scent of rosemary, thyme and lavender thick in the air. Blake was asking for more than Sloane thought she could give. She hadn't wanted anything for herself in a long time, hadn't dared to hope. But Blake wasn't asking for promises—she was just asking if Sloane was willing to try, to imagine a future they could build together.

And that was terrifying.

CHAPTER FIFTEEN

Blake

BLAKE TOOK THE time to read over her notes from the week at the resort. There were a few pages she could use for the article. She had a collection of images, pages of handwritten notes, and she spent a few hours forming them into something readable before getting ready for the grand opening reception.

She sent them off to Tara with a brief outline for the article. She hoped it was enough to piece together when she got back. Now she had two stories. The messy, vulnerable truths scribbled into the margins of her notebook. And the polished, refined notes of a glamorous week in Napa. Neither felt complete. They were two halves of the same story. The best week of her life, the most complicated week of her life.

And she wasn't sure how Tara would react to the half she had sent. But she didn't have time to think about that now. She was already late for the culminating event of her week at Vella West: the Grand Opening Gala.

Blake had been nervous about tonight the entire week. Large crowds made her anxious, especially because she wouldn't know anyone. As PR manager, Robby invited the who's who of Napa Valley, San Francisco and beyond to debut the large reception area. She knew it would be lavish, and gorgeous and overwhelming in the best way.

She also knew this was it. After tonight, she returned to San Diego. She'd be saying goodbye to Sloane, to Robby, to Winnie and Rhett. And she wasn't ready.

As Blake stepped onto the smooth stone of the Vella West pavilion, the hand-laid tiles cool beneath her feet, she took a deep breath. She was done up in an ethereal blue dress that clung to her hips and strappy heels she would never have chosen herself, yet were somehow perfect for the elegant space. She knew this moment would forever be etched in her memory; a blend of unexpected harmony and unforgettable beauty.

Blake had wandered this terrace a dozen times over the past week, memorizing its lines, its angles, the way the light stretched across the stone in the late afternoon—but tonight, it was unrecognizable. Gauzy drapes caught the breeze like sails, casting fleeting shadows across the vineyard view. Lanterns flickered from the low branches of the old oaks, their golden glow warming Sloane's face as she chatted with someone across the terrace. Music drifted—low, lilting, familiar—and for a moment, Blake couldn't tell if it was the melody or Sloane's smile that made her chest tighten. The scent of night-blooming jasmine curled around them, and beneath it, the earthy sweetness of ripening grapes.

And above all, the people. There had to be hundreds—gliding through sunset-dappled courtyards and lingering beneath the branches of old oaks. The crowd was a curated kind of eclectic: soft linen trousers paired with vintage leather boots, silk skirts brushing the tops of scuffed Converse, wide-brimmed hats worn without irony. There were floaty dresses in desert pinks, sharp suits in rumpled cotton, bold prints that clashed just enough to feel intentional. Hair in every shape—slicked back, coiled in buns, left wild from the wind—framed faces that radiated ease. Northern California through and through. A little bohemian, a little luxury, all of it worn with ease.

Blake scanned the scene, a knot tightening just below her ribs. Everyone looked so effortlessly at home, as if they belonged here—laughing over glasses of pinot noir and chardonnay, all made from Vella West vineyards.

Every hand held a stemmed glass, every smile seemed real. And for a moment, she wondered if she could belong here, too.

It had been less than a week since Sloane reentered her life, and already she was imagining them tangled up together again. Blake couldn't—wouldn't—be the one to ask. Yesterday, she'd asked Sloane to think about what she wanted. Blake could only hope that Sloane had listened. If Sloane wanted something with Blake, she was going to have to be the one to say it. Blake wasn't about to risk another rejection. Her heart wouldn't survive it a second time.

She searched for Sloane in the crowd, hoping she could find some kind of confirmation of Sloane's feelings with a look or a smile, when another person caught her attention. Blake had seen him earlier in the week, just once—from a distance, talking with Sloane around the horse stable. She hadn't expected to see him again tonight, let alone here, lingering near the edge of the lantern-lit terrace in a suit that looked custom tailored for his frame. He couldn't have been over twenty, with the boyish, unfinished look of someone still growing into himself, the kind of kid who tried to stand straighter when someone looked his way.

While everyone else looked dolled up for the night, he seemed at ease. His hair flopped to one side, and just the right amount of ankle flashed between the bottom of his pants and the cognac leather oxfords. But when he turned and the terrace lights caught his face, Blake felt the recognition land sharp and strange in her chest. The eyes. Dark as midnight, thoughtful, unmistakably Sloane's.

Nico, she realized. It had to be. Sloane had said she wanted to introduce them, but everything had gotten so hectic. The resemblance was too strong. And suddenly, in this dreamlike version of the place she thought she'd come to know, Blake felt time fold in on itself—past and present brushing close enough to stir something she wasn't ready for.

Her indignation with Sloane softened as she took in the way she cared for him. She wrapped herself around him almost protectively. He must have been so young. Probably still in elementary school when Sloane had become his guardian. This whole time Blake had been picturing a peer for Sloane. Maybe someone a few years younger. But this kid, he was a kid truly, looked at Sloane as if she hung the moon.

Sloane had shattered her heart. Given the way her chest ached now, she knew she'd always treat it like a healed break, covering it instinctively if danger came too close. Sloane hadn't meant to cause all this pain—she knew that now—but the ache couldn't be helped.

Maybe there was a part of Sloane that was still aching, too.

Blake wanted to run to her. To tell her she was sorry. That of course Sloane had done what she needed to do to survive. She wanted her to know she was proud of her, and proud to know her, in any capacity Sloane would have her.

Although she hoped it would be more. She wanted more.

Blake's heart cracked open with a sudden, brutal clarity: She was still in love with Sloane. Sloane, who was kind and selfless and always trying so hard to do the right thing. Sloane, who had shattered her heart in the name of someone else's healing. Blake wanted to go to her, to hold her, to say she was ready for whatever came next.

But the thought stopped her. Because whatever came next could be the moment it all fell apart again. She loved Sloane. That much was undeniable. And she understood why Sloane had left. She could trace every choice, every fear, and still it didn't quiet the ache that had taken root in her chest. Understanding didn't fix it. And love didn't protect anything. It only made the pain more precise.

Her heart pulled toward Sloane, desperate to

close the distance and speak all the things she'd buried just to stay standing. But beneath that urgency, something colder anchored her in place. Because opening herself up again meant risking everything.

But before she could decide, Nico was walking toward her. Arms outstretched and smile wide. She braced herself for impact.

"You must be Blake," he said with a smile. A perfect smile. Sloane's smile. "I'm Nico, Sloane's cousin."

Blake held out her hand and shook his. "It's so nice to meet you," Blake said, her heart in her throat.

"Yeah, it's nice to meet you, too. Sloane wasn't going to tell me who you were, but I recognized you from your picture." He squinted at her and nodded. "You look the same. Plus, when you walked in and her eyes went all—" he held his hands up in front of his own eyes and mimicked little fireworks "—she didn't have to tell me."

"Oh!" Blake was a bit taken aback with how open and honest this kid was. Not at all like the Sloane she'd first met. Not at all standoffish. Maybe this was what having a loving and supportive parent figure did for someone? "Thank you?"

"For sure," he said. Nico exuded an aura of boundless loyalty and good cheer, like a golden retriever, all sunshine and warmth. Big smile, bright eyes, easily distracted. "Oh, look. They have my favorite." He motioned toward a woman with a larger platter. "These ones, with the little pieces of truffle and the fig jam. They're the best."

He took a napkin and placed four crostini haphazardly into his hand. The server smiled patiently before leaving, presumably to refill their tray. He held one out to Blake, but she waved him off. There was no way she was going to stand between Nico and his crostini.

He happily chomped down on the toasted bread before saying, "But I just wanted to introduce myself. And say thanks for being so cool about Sloane."

"I am very cool."

"Yeah, I told her not to come, but she told me that since I've never been before she wants to make sure I get settled."

Blake's brain whirled with so many questions. "I don't mind," she said, with absolutely no idea what he was talking about.

"I even told her to bring you with us, but she said no. I'm sure you have a bunch of stuff going on anyway. Who wants to repeat their European vacation with their kid cousin tagging along, right?" He rolled his eyes. "If you change your mind, I'm not that bad. I promise."

Blake's whole world whirled around her. Sloane was leaving for Europe? And she didn't want Blake to come with. Not that Blake expected Sloane to invite her. It wasn't like they were together. Even so, it stung to know they'd spent the entire week together and not once had Sloane mentioned travel.

"Sloane is going back to Europe?"

Nico shoved yet another crostini in his mouth and nodded as he chewed. "Yeah, I have an internship there this summer for viticulture." He held out a crostini to Blake and she waved it away. She couldn't eat anything. Not now.

She'd asked Sloane to take some time, to think about what their future could be. And she hadn't even mentioned a big trip. How were they ever going to have a chance at a future if she couldn't be honest with her. It wasn't the fact that she was leaving. It was the fact that, yet again, Sloane was leaving her in the dark. Prioritizing her own self-preservation over something they might build together.

Blake thought they'd had some kind of breakthrough in the secret garden. Sloane had been real and honest with her—or so she thought. Maybe she'd just been building up to the moment she'd leave again.

"I'm sure the two of you will have a great

time," she said. She took a shaky breath and a sip of white wine, but she didn't taste it at all.

"Yeah, it's going to be great. But for real, I've never seen Sloane this distracted. And I mean that in a good way. She's usually all *work, work, papers, frown.* I think last night was the first time she's ever just…taken the night off." Nico looked almost dazed as he counted back in his mind. "It was kind of cool. And Robby totally handled it."

"I think you lost me," Blake admitted. This kid was hard to keep up with. Her brain was still fixated on this trip to Europe that Sloane had failed to mention. She felt her whole body tense with frustration.

"Never mind—it's all good. I need to go find more snacks." His eyes roamed the open space in search of another server. Blake was still trying to figure out the last thing he said. "Promise I'll get to say goodbye before I head out tomorrow."

"I will try. I'm heading out tomorrow, too," Blake said. She had regretted the early morning flight, but maybe now it was a good thing.

"Wait. You're leaving? Already?"

"Yeah, I live in San Diego. I'm just up here for work. For the article."

Nico frowned and looked Blake up and down like he didn't believe a word she said. "Well, I guess you better go find Sloane now then."

And with that, Nico waved and jogged off to a young woman in black pants and a crisp white shirt, holding a tray of tiny glass cups filled with a rainbow smattering of crudités.

Blake didn't want to be the person standing alone at a glamorous party, so she took off toward the outskirts of the pavilion, hoping a walk near the flowers would ease her racing mind.

Sloane

Nico was up to no good. Sloane could tell from the lopsided grin and the way he kept flirting with one of the catering staff. She'd have to talk to him later about expectations. He was an adult and he'd have to start behaving that way. At least occasionally.

Listen to her. She sounded like her parents. No. She sounded like *a* parent. There was a difference.

And she was a parent in many ways, she supposed. Raising someone for ten years, even if they weren't *yours*, certainly meant something.

"Boss, this is all brilliant. Well done." Robby came to a stop next to Sloane and tipped their wineglass to her.

Sloane pressed her lips together. "It's Sloane. And we both know this event was all you. Especially last night. Thank you for handling the caterers last minute. And the electrical issues in the Hyacinth Cottage."

"Of course."

"Even if it did mean moving Nico into my tiny house."

Sloane had not been happy to come home after midnight and discover her cousin snoring on her couch. If she had known he would stay with her, she would have fixed up a proper bed. He'd requested a room at the resort so he could be close to the gym and the pool. But Robby hadn't set one aside for him since technically he wasn't supposed to be here for another few weeks.

But she'd taken one look at the six-foot water polo player on her couch and sighed before rousing him and moving him to her bed. Then she'd made up the couch and slept there herself. She still had the crick in her neck to prove it.

"Perhaps tonight, *you* could find a different room?"

When Sloane looked at Robby, their eyebrows were practically flying away. "Robby. I don't know what you're talking about."

"Oh, please, boss. Anyone can see the two of you are smitten with each other. And I was wrong. When I told you to be careful. She's clearly in love with you. And don't think I didn't do some detective work. That's *her*, right? She is the woman from the summer that—"

"I don't want to talk about it, Robby. That summer was a long time ago." When Sloane had taken over guardianship of Nico, she'd needed help. She was still finishing grad school, trying to juggle so many things, and Robby had answered an ad for a personal assistant. They were still in college, underqualified, blew the interview and crashed into a planter in the front yard. But they'd also made Nico laugh for the first time in months.

Sloane hired them on the spot. And then got them the training they needed.

"Frankly, boss, I don't care what you want. You saw something in me ten years ago. You gave me a job, you encouraged me to grow and now I get to manage PR at a world-class resort."

"And you're qualified to do it."

"I know, but that is not the point. The point is, let me return the favor. I see something in you, when you're with her. She brings you to life in a way I've never seen before. If you have even a small chance to keep this going, you have to try. You deserve to be happy. You deserve to go after the things you want."

"Even if I wanted it… I'm not ready. You heard Nico. He got into his internship program. In less than a month he's leaving. He needs me. I can't just—"

Robby silenced Sloane with one pointed stare.

"Taking a few weeks off to go to Europe is not an insurmountable challenge. Nico wants you to be happy. Your uncle would want you to be happy."

Sloane took a deep shaky breath and swiped at a tear. Nico *needed* her. She couldn't let him down. Not the way her own parents had let her down when they dismissed her sexuality and her dreams. This was a chance for her to get it right. "I just want to do right by him. I want him to know I'll always be there."

"And you will be, but he's twenty-two now. And you're only thirty-two. It's okay. Let her in."

Sloane nodded once. She thought of all the things she'd been through in the last ten years. Taking over guardianship. Overseeing her uncle's estate until it could become her cousin's. Knowing she was thrust into a world where she wasn't sure she belonged. Knowing she had a million things to prove.

She'd been strategic with investments, she'd done her part, and then she leveraged them to open this resort. And in four years, he would be twenty-five. He would get his inheritance. And then maybe he wouldn't need her anymore. At least not in the same way.

And it also filled her with hope. Nico was an adult now. He'd always need her, but not in the same way, not as much. And admitting that meant admitting she *could* be with Blake—if she was willing to fight for her.

But the thought of losing Blake. Again. After how they'd reconnected? That was just as unbearable. Was it possible that there could be a world where she could have it all? She could be there for Nico, take care of this resort and make room in her for life for Blake?

"Maybe you should go talk to her, before she goes?"

"What are you talking about?"

Sloane's eyes snapped up and she searched for Blake in the crowd. But all she saw was golden brown curls bouncing up and down as Blake left the party.

CHAPTER SIXTEEN

Blake

BLAKE GRIMACED AS she made her way along the lavender path and back to her cottage. The broken heel of her strappy sandal dangled pathetically in her hands. She should have known better than to wear these shoes in the uneven terrain. But they'd gone perfectly with the dress Sloane had sent her earlier in the week, and she couldn't resist. It was worth her current hobbling situation.

And, she had to admit, the wardrobe malfunction did give her an excuse to step away for a moment. Nico hadn't held back when he'd told her all about Sloane's plans to leave town. She was still reeling from the news when a group of partygoers had accosted her with questions about the resort and her connection to it. Blake had felt the creep of embarrassment in her cheeks when she remembered that technically her connection was through her employer, *Elsewhere Magazine*.

The group had *loved* that. They had tons of recommendations, many for their own vineyards or businesses, and Blake wasn't sure how to handle the attention. She was used to being behind the camera, behind a screen, not people-ing at a grand gala.

Blake had worried she wouldn't fit in tonight. Sloane's friends were used to the polished, sun-soaked world of Napa's luxury resorts, with their manicured vineyards and carefully orchestrated parties. Maybe she was just a stranger who'd stumbled into Sloane's life ten years too late, an uninvited ripple in waters Sloane had fought so hard to calm.

Blake's thoughts churned, heavy and tangled. *You showed up ten years later at a resort she created based on memories of you.* The thought echoed inside her chest, complicated and aching. But Sloane's life was messy. Wrapped in layers Blake hadn't yet fully peeled back. Sloane had carried so much for so many years—all on her own. And she wasn't ready to let Blake help. Blake wasn't going to be the one chasing or pleading. She was the one who'd come back, unexpectedly, and maybe that made her the intruder. The one who had to respect the walls Sloane needed to keep up for now.

Lost in those swirling thoughts as she sat on the edge of her bed, Blake barely noticed the knock at her door until it pulled her back, sharp and urgent. She blinked and opened the door without bothering to check who was knocking. And there she was.

Sloane.

Disheveled. Eyes wild and trembling like a storm barely contained. Her usually sleek bob was windblown and messy, and every movement thrummed with desperate energy.

"You left the party," Sloane said, voice breathless, stepping inside as though she couldn't bear to let Blake escape. "I don't know what I did to upset you, but please—I'll make it right. Tell me what's wrong."

Blake's chest tightened at the raw vulnerability in Sloane's voice. This wasn't the poised, guarded woman she'd known earlier, but someone real—fractured, but wanting to be understood.

"Sloane, slow down," Blake said gently, reaching out, her hand brushing Sloane's arm, stilling the trembling in her hands. "It's okay."

"It's not okay." Sloane's words rushed out in a near whisper, a jagged edge to her tone. "You show up to the grand opening, wearing that dress—" Sloane's eyes dipped to Blake's waist for a moment.

Blake bit the edge of her lip. She hadn't worn the dress originally because she didn't want

Sloane to think she could be bought. But when she'd finally unzipped the garment bag this morning, she knew she couldn't leave without at least trying it on.

"Do you like it?" Blake asked.

"It's gorgeous. *You're* gorgeous. But that's not the point." Sloane shoved a hand through her hair. She stared off in the distance as she seemed to reorganize her thoughts. "Dammit, Blake. I don't want you to go. I'm a mess. A giant mess with a million things I don't know how to fix. But if you're okay with messes..." Her voice cracked, a shaky, hopeful smile breaking through. "I kind of think you are. Please don't go."

Blake's heart stuttered, her breath hitching. Sloane's confession felt like being swept into the air in the world's biggest hot-air balloon, yet there was something raw and familiar in it—something that made her want to pull Sloane close, to ease the ache in her voice. But she didn't move.

Instead, Blake laughed softly, a nervous sound, caught somewhere between disbelief and relief. She'd waited ten years for this. And this was how Sloane found her. Barefoot and considering the best way to leave.

She held up her broken shoe, the heel swinging limply in the air like a fragile flag.

"My shoe broke when I stepped off the lavender path," Blake said, voice softer than she intended. "I came back to change. But, Sloane… you…want me to stay?"

Sloane's cheeks flushed bright. Her eyes flicked down to the shoe, then back to Blake, her gaze unreadable for a second too long. Finally, she cleared her throat, a nervous chuckle escaping her lips. "Oh. Your shoe. That's… I see. Your shoe." She quickly tried to recover. "We can just go back to the party now."

Blake shook her head, the smile widening despite the tug of vulnerability in her chest. She stepped closer to Sloane, feeling the gravity of the moment pull tight between them. There was something trembling in Sloane's eyes now, something unsure. And Blake's heart—her heart that had been full of *doubt* and *fear* for so long—felt soft and open.

"Sloane," Blake whispered. "Look at me."

The air seemed to shift. Time itself seemed to hold its breath. Sloane leaned back against the door frame, small and vulnerable—like Cinderella just before midnight, like the magic might slip away any second.

Sloane's eyes met hers, shimmering with unshed tears, blinking rapidly to hold herself steady. "Of course, I want you to stay," she whispered, her voice so quiet, it felt as though it could break. “I’ve always wanted you with me, even when I didn’t know how to be. Even when I was so lost in all this…all this mess. And now I’m terrified you’ll leave. That I’ll lose you again. But maybe that’s just me. Maybe I’m too broken to let anyone close. But *you*—you’re worth the risk, Blake. You’re worth all of it.”

Blake’s breath caught, the weight of Sloane’s words making her heart skip like smooth stones across water before finally sinking in. It was too much, and yet, somehow, it was everything. She stepped closer, closing the remaining distance between them until the air was thick with unspoken tension. She could feel Sloane’s pulse under her skin, her body trembling slightly as though the world outside might come crashing in at any moment.

“Don’t be scared,” Blake murmured, her lips barely brushing Sloane’s forehead. “You don’t have to be perfect, Sloane. I never needed perfect.”

Sloane let out a shaky breath, her hand trembling as she reached up, threading her fingers through Blake’s hair.

“You don’t understand,” Sloane said softly, voice breaking. “I did have to be perfect. Nico deserves perfect. My uncle should still be here. But he’s not. And it’s my job to hold all of it together. It’s my job to make sure his legacy continues.”

"Is that why you're leaving?" Blake asked, her voice soft as silk.

"Leaving?"

"For Europe. Nico told me you're leaving with him." Blake worked to keep her voice calm. She had no right to be mad about it. Sloane could go wherever she wanted. Sloane *should* go with Nico. Even if Sloane leaving again, leaving *Blake* again, was the exact thing she was trying to protect herself from. Blake's heart crumbled to pieces in her chest, but she kept her chin from wobbling, and she was proud of that.

Sloane blinked. "He told you that?"

That wasn't a no. Blake got the next words out even if they hurt. "Yes. And he asked me to go, too." She choked out a breathy laugh. "I can see now how you've had your hands full with him."

Sloane took in a shuddering breath, her shoulders dropping. "Yeah, I hope I'm doing it right. I know I'm not my uncle. I could never be. But I want to do right by him."

Blake reached up, gently cupping Sloane's face, grounding her in the moment. "It's not your job to be your uncle. You get to decide how this all happens. You get to decide what you want."

"I'm sorry I didn't tell you," Sloane said as she leaned into Blake's touch. "I just found out, nothing has been decided. And I just—"

Blake reached forward and wiped at a tear

threatening to spill over Sloane's lashes. Sloane sniffed and nodded. Blake stepped closer, the space between them evaporating in an instant. She closed the gap, pressing her lips gently to Sloane's mouth. It was a kiss that spoke of years of silence, the burning need to *finally* let go, the longing to believe in something real.

Because this was real. Even if it was messy and they were still figuring it all out. This week had been a gift. A precious slip back in time. Blake had Sloane in her arms, and she was real and soft and hard at the edges, and Blake intended to keep her there.

"It's okay, Sloane." Another kiss to her cheek. "It's okay." And to her temple. Her hairline. And back to her mouth. "We're okay. We can figure it all out."

It wasn't rushed. It wasn't frantic. It was slow, tender and full of every ounce of emotion neither of them had allowed themselves to feel. Blake's arms slid around Sloane's back, pulling her closer, feeling the tremble in Sloane's body.

Sloane

Later, Blake led Sloane out onto the secluded wooden porch of her cottage. The night air was cool and crisp, a gentle breeze rustling through the nearby olive trees, their silvery leaves shimmering faintly under the moonlight. It was the kind of night that felt suspended, as if time itself had slowed down just to let them exist in it, just the two of them.

In the distance, the party carried on—a murmur of laughter, clinking glasses and the steady rhythm of the live band filtering softly through the dark. But here, on the private terrace, there was only the quiet hum of the evening and the warmth of the space surrounding them. The world felt far away, and yet it felt as if it were pressing close, holding its breath.

The bungalow felt like a world apart—quiet, intimate, a sanctuary from everything swirling inside Sloane's head. She had spent so much of the last few years fighting to keep everything under control, to manage every moment, every decision, with perfect precision. But here, with Blake beside her, that constant need to *control* seemed to dissolve, like the last traces of daylight slipping away into night.

The warm glow from the porch light cast soft shadows over Blake's face, highlighting the vulnerability and strength Sloane saw there. Blake was always so open, so unafraid to be seen. It made something inside Sloane ache—something she had hidden deep, tucked away under layers of duty and responsibility.

"Do you want to go back to the party?" Blake

asked, her voice low, almost hesitant. There was an edge of uncertainty to her, as if she was afraid that maybe she was pushing too much, too soon.

Sloane shook her head slowly, her eyes fixed on the fading lights of the resort below. The laughter, the music, the buzz of the crowd—they all seemed so distant now, like echoes from another world. "Not right now," she whispered, the words barely more than breath. It felt like an admission. A release. She didn't need the noise. She didn't need the spectacle. Not when she could feel Blake's presence next to her, steady and warm, like the first light of dawn after a long, dark night.

Blake moved closer, sitting down beside her, the motion fluid, instinctive. She leaned gently onto Sloane's shoulder, the weight of her touch soft but firm, a quiet reassurance that no matter the mess or the chaos, she wasn't alone.

Sloane let herself settle into the moment, the weight of Blake's presence anchoring her. It was simple, this closeness, and yet it was everything. It was the first thing that felt real in a long time.

"I think I know what I'm going to write for my article," Blake said softly, as if sharing a secret, her voice just loud enough to reach Sloane's ear.

Sloane glanced up at her, surprise softening her features. She had thought Blake would be too caught up in the celebration to even think about work. "But your stay isn't finished. I was still planning to wow you with the resort's brunch tomorrow."

Blake shrugged, a shy smile tugging at her lips, the corners of her mouth lifting in a way that made Sloane's heart beat just a little faster. "It's already done. When you know, you know."

And Sloane *did* know. She knew it in the way Blake's eyes lingered on her, the way she didn't rush to fill the silence, the way her mere presence calmed the storm inside. For the first time, Sloane understood that there was no real need for grand gestures or promises. She didn't need a private train car or an entire morning sky. This quiet moment was enough. The honesty, the rawness of just being in each other's space—it was more than enough. It was everything.

Sloane's chest tightened, a rush of emotion flooding through her. It was fierce, tender—something sharp and soft all at once. She reached out, her fingers brushing lightly against Blake's cheek, feeling the warmth of her skin. And then, slowly, as if the very act of moving closer required all of her courage, she pressed her lips to Blake's in a kiss.

It was slow, deliberate, full of promise and quiet determination. There was no rush. No need to prove anything. Whatever storms they still had to weather, whatever fears or doubts remained, they would face them side by side. Together.

The kiss lingered—soft and full of everything that had remained unspoken. It was the kind of kiss that made the rest of the world fade into the background, until all that mattered was the warmth between them, the steady rhythm of their hearts and the hopeful silence of the night around them.

When they finally pulled away, neither of them moved far. They stayed close, shoulders brushing, sharing a silence that was deeper than words. Outside, the music still drifted faintly through the cool night air, but here, in this moment, there was only them. The party could wait. The world could wait.

For now, this was all they needed.

CHAPTER SEVENTEEN

Blake

SUNLIGHT SPILLED ACROSS the honeymoon cottage in thick, golden ribbons. It pooled on the floor, warmed the sheets, caught in the loose ends of Sloane's hair. Blake stirred slowly, then all at once, blinking into morning with the sudden, full-body awareness that she wasn't alone.

Sloane was pressed against her, still asleep. Her breathing deep and even. Her face turned slightly toward Blake's shoulder. Their legs tangled beneath the sheets like they'd been searching for each other even in sleep.

She hadn't slept like this in years. Not next to someone. Not safely. Not like her body had finally remembered what peace felt like.

Sloane didn't stir when Blake moved, didn't even flinch as Blake gently extricated herself from the bed. She was such a heavy sleeper. That hadn't changed. Blake smiled to herself—little forgotten memories of Sloane returning now in fragments. The way she hogged blankets. The way she muttered nonsense when nudged awake. The way she kissed like it meant something.

Blake pressed a kiss to Sloane's temple and padded to the door, expecting to find the usual silver tray waiting in the hall. She braced herself for the scent of tea and citrus scones, for the single flower in a bud vase, delicate and fragrant.

Except today, there was nothing.

No tray. No flower. Just a quiet, empty hallway.

"That's odd," she murmured, frowning as she stepped back inside.

Sloane was awake now, still lounging lazily beneath the sheets, one arm tucked beneath her head, the other thrown wide like she owned the room. The morning light made her skin look like marble and gold. Blake tried not to stare. Failed.

"What's odd?" Sloane asked, eyes soft with sleep.

"The breakfast tray," Blake said, confused. "It's not here. They've brought it every morning like clockwork. Always the same—fruit, pastries, Earl Grey with cream. And the flowers... they're this haphazard mishmash of the most gorgeous wildflowers. But somehow, it works?"

Sloane was quiet.

Blake looked at her. "What?"

Sloane let out a slow breath. "We don't have a breakfast service, Blake."

Blake blinked. "What do you mean?"

"I mean…there's no one delivering those trays. That was me."

The world tilted.

Blake stared at her. "What?"

"I know you like Earl Grey," Sloane said softly, almost like it was a confession. "And you hate melon. And you always loved lavender shortbread. I just thought… I don't know. I wanted your mornings here to feel good. Even before…everything else."

Blake sat slowly at the foot of the bed, as if her legs couldn't be trusted to keep holding her up. Her throat tightened.

"You were doing that even before we talked. Before we figured anything out. Before I knew you even wanted me here."

Sloane nodded, looking suddenly shy. "I wasn't sure if you'd stay. But I knew you'd wake up."

Blake let out a shaky breath. Her vision blurred. "You brought me breakfast. Every morning?"

Sloane nodded again, quieter this time. "With flowers. From my garden. You used to pick them in Florence. I remembered that."

The flood hit Blake all at once—memories, feelings, the impossibly tender ache of being known so completely by someone she thought she'd lost. Her chest ached in a way that felt both sharp and astonishingly good. Like something healing beneath the skin.

"You didn't owe me anything," Blake whispered. "You could've ignored me. You should have."

"I didn't want to ignore you," Sloane said simply. "I wanted to show up for you. I didn't know how else to say it yet."

Blake pressed her hands over her mouth, overcome. The breakfasts, the tea, the lavender—she had thought it was just hospitality. Some polished luxury offered to all guests. But it had been Sloane. It had always been her.

All those mornings…before the apologies. Before the kisses. Before they were even speaking fully like people who used to be in love.

She wasn't sure if she wanted to cry or laugh or climb back into bed and never leave.

"God, Sloane," she said, voice breaking. "You were already taking care of me. And I didn't even know."

Sloane reached forward, gently hooking her fingers around Blake's wrist and tugging her closer. "I've always wanted to. Even when I didn't know how."

Blake leaned in, their foreheads resting together. "I still can't believe you remember how I take my tea."

"Too much cream. No sugar. Always Earl

Grey." Sloane grinned. "You used to dip your toast in it. Like a heathen."

"Still do."

Sloane tilted her head. "Come back to bed."

Blake nodded; eyes still glossy with unshed tears. She slid beneath the covers again, curling into Sloane like it was instinct, like she had never left at all.

"I can't believe it was you," she whispered again.

"You believe it now?"

Blake smiled against her shoulder. "I believe everything now."

And they stayed that way, skin to skin, breath to breath, as the sun climbed higher. Breakfast could wait. The rest of the world could wait. But this—this quiet, powerful truth—was finally here.

Sloane

This was why brunch existed—because it was almost noon, but Sloane could still order an omelet and drink something sparkly in public.

The morning air was soft around the poolside patio, dappled through pale umbrellas, scented with rosemary and citrus, and punctuated by the gentle murmur of other guests enjoying their last hours of the weekend. A server had just dropped off a new pot of Earl Grey, and across the table, Blake was stirring in cream—her hair still damp from a shower, face clean and open, bare feet tucked beneath her chair.

Sloane barely touched her mimosa.

The *Santa Ynez Valley Chronicle* lay folded in front of her, creased where she'd been gripping it too tightly.

"Vella West Grand Opening: Boutique Luxury with Heart and Vision."

They'd written a glowing feature, more expansive than she'd expected. It praised everything—architecture, wine, staff, food—but it was the final paragraph that got her. The writer described the resort as *a place you could come to feel like yourself again. A home, dressed in elegance.* It was the kind of praise she'd dreamed of.

And it didn't mean a thing without someone to share it with.

She stole a glance across the table at Blake. Her sleeves were rolled, a gold ring glinting faintly on her middle finger as she cradled the teacup. A familiar ache tightened behind Sloane's ribs. She knew Blake had to leave today, but she couldn't escape the desire to move that tiny band of gold one finger over, asking her to stay forever.

But before she could get carried away, Blake's phone chirped on the table between them—a terrible reminder that life still had obstacles for them, even though they seemed to be on the same page for the first time in ten years.

Blake tapped something out on the phone. “My car. I told the hotel to send it at one. I totally lost track of time.”

“Wait,” Sloane said. “Can’t you push it? Just an hour?” She needed more. She’d offer to charter a plane for Blake if she thought she’d accept it. She’d offer to go with if she thought she could get away with it. Blake had her entire heart—and it was going to be torture to live without it until they got this all sorted.

Blake stood. “I wish I could. I’ve got a debrief call with my editor as soon as I land, and a meeting first thing tomorrow. I wasn’t even supposed to stay this long.”

Sloane stood, too. “I thought we had more time.”

Blake’s voice softened. “I did, too.”

Sloane looked at her, really looked—at the shadows under her eyes, the hopeful pink of her cheeks.

“I’ll walk you to the car.”

They didn’t speak much as they headed through the garden path, past the vines and wildflowers, the scent of lavender caught on the breeze. Guests were checking out, the world moving forward while Sloane wanted time to stop.

Outside the front entrance, the town car waited. Blake's bag was already loaded. The driver leaned on the hood, scrolling through his phone.

Blake turned to her. "I'm glad I came."

Sloane nodded, but her voice caught. "I wish you didn't have to leave."

"I wish I didn't either."

They stared at each other. The moment a breath away from cracking open.

Then Blake stepped forward and pulled her into a hug—longer than expected, her face pressed into the crook of Sloane's neck. Sloane wrapped her arms around her waist and held on.

"I don't want this to be the end," Sloane said, the words thick in her throat.

Blake leaned back just far enough to look her in the eye. "Then don't let it be. Think about what you want. Think about what you're willing to give. And then find me. We both have things we need to take care of. I'll be waiting for you."

Sloane kissed her. Just once—soft and lingering. Something slow enough to say what she couldn't.

"I'm not trying to fix everything. I just don't want this to be another goodbye. I don't want to wait another ten years."

"You need to finish opening this resort. Robby needs you, the town needs you. And I need to figure out my next steps with writing. This isn't goodbye. This is…pause."

Sloane bit back tears as she pressed her forehead to Blake's. "Okay." She wrapped her in a hug. She knew she was right. They weren't twenty anymore. They had responsibilities and things that needed sorting out. They couldn't just run away together.

But it still scraped her heart out to watch Blake Miller drive away.

CHAPTER EIGHTEEN

Blake

BLAKE KNEW COMING home was going to be hard, but it wasn't in the ways she'd imagined. She sat down at her laptop, ready to finalize her edits in preparation for the meeting the next day.

Her apartment was compact. Okay fine, it was small. Probably not much bigger than the honeymoon cottage she'd spent the last week in. But it also felt flat. Her home didn't have any photographs adorning the walls. She had some prints of local places, but nothing she could look at and pinpoint to a memory.

Not like Sloane's small home, full of pictures of Nico and her uncle from every stage of life. She didn't even have an old photo of her and Sloane. Not mismatched mugs or hand-stitched quilts.

Blake sighed and opened her laptop. She had a million notifications on her work's social media. She opened it as a way to ease back into work.

She'd address a few comments and upload a few final photos before turning to her write-up of the resort.

She clicked on the home icon and her website flooded with vibrant images from the past week. To any stranger these photos would look like a luxurious stay in the bespoke vineyards of the Napa Valley. A farm to table breakfast tray, the sunrise over the hills from hundreds of feet in the air, a picnic in a meadow with homemade jams.

Catchy phrases and targeted hashtags accompanied each photograph, subtly advertising the resort and related products while appealing to those seeking adventure, luxury and travel escapes.

But there were other hints there, too. A hazy, backlit photo showed Sloane's form leaning against the railing of the honeymoon cottage, her features lost in shadow. No one would know it was her. Winnie and Rhett in their corral, noses together in the midday sun. Blake's novel splayed open at the foot of her lounge chair in a cabana. She'd tried different captions here. Lines from her journal. Snippets of poems half remembered. She'd snuck them in between advertisements disguised as art.

Her heart caught in her throat as she read the comments. People wanted more. She thought she'd been capturing small moments, but she had told a story in photos. She'd let the world watch her slowly fall back in love over the course of the last week.

Her followers had noticed. *Who is that woman in the photo?* And *since when did you start writing poetry?* The edge of her journal peeked out in a photo. Blake had let people in, a lot of people in, without realizing it.

Blake tapped her pen against her mouth and frowned. She had almost finished the write-up. But she knew there was another story here. She scrolled through the comments again. She liked them all and responded to some, each response a tiny hot-air balloon of hope in her chest.

Her phone buzzed beside her and she happily answered when she saw Chloe's name.

"Welcome home, Blake!" Chloe's chipper voice rang out on the other side of the line. Blake didn't have a chance to respond before Chloe plowed through the conversation. "We are meeting on Friday for coffee at nine. You can't say no. I want to know all about the mystery woman on your feed. You didn't tell me you *met someone* on the trip. Who is she? Another guest? I need *details*."

Chloe's voice, a familiar and slightly chaotic melody, reached Blake's ears, reminding her that she wasn't completely alone in San Diego. Even if she hadn't realized it until now. And even if that friend was a bit overbearing, it was nice to know she had someone she could talk to.

"Actually, I was wondering if Tara had time to squeeze in a meeting with me on Friday?" Blake tried to keep her voice steady. "I want to talk to her about the article. But we can get breakfast afterward?"

"You don't have it, do you?" Chloe's voice dropped to a whisper. "Oh god, we're all getting fired. I can't work at Java Bean again, Blake."

Blake stifled a laugh. "Don't turn in any applications just yet. I have the article. But there's something else I want to show Tara, too. And I'd like to meet with her about it."

"Okay, I can do tomorrow morning before her first meeting. Bring her an oat latte. It will loosen her up a little."

"Thanks, Chloe. You're the best."

With that, Blake hung up and pulled out her tattered notebook with thousands of words already penned. It was time to finally let it all out. It was time to tell her story. Sloane's story.

That Friday, Blake sat stiffly in the high-backed chair across from Tara's desk, the tips of her fingers tapping nervously against her blazer. Her hair was pulled back into a tight ponytail—sleek, controlled, the antithesis of the woman she had been when she'd first stepped into the world of travel writing.

She glanced around the office, feeling the weight of it all—white walls, chrome furniture, an overstuffed bookshelf filled with trade magazines and bound volumes of past issues. Tara's domain was always immaculate, the kind of place where everything had its place. Everything was curated, even the air. Blake hated it. The space was sterile. The office felt as devoid of warmth as she felt inside.

Once, she'd been excited about this job, eager to write about new places, experiences and the world beyond her cubicle. But now, months later, she could barely recognize the person who had walked into this building with wide eyes and an open heart. She'd given up parts of herself to fit the role. The work was fine. The job was fine. But Blake didn't feel *right* anymore.

She was the magazine's social media manager. She posted; she curated content; she engaged with followers. It was supposed to be her way in—the backdoor to the writer's room, the place where her real ambitions lived. Tara had promised her that if she proved herself, if she could show her potential, she might just get a shot at writing those glossy travel pieces.

But now Blake knew something—*really* knew

something—that she hadn't before. She wasn't meant to be here. Not like this. Not doing this.

Tara finally looked up from the draft of Blake's latest article, her sharp eyes scanning Blake with the practiced gaze of someone who could read the room in a heartbeat. Tara didn't waste time with pleasantries or unearned compliments. She was precise, concise and ruthless when it came to business. It wasn't personal. It never was with Tara.

"Blake, I asked you to write a travel review," Tara said, her voice smooth, devoid of inflection. "I trust that's what you have for me?"

"Tara, I—" Blake was great at writing words down, but not so great when she had to say them out loud, on the spot, to her boss. "I did write one. And it was *fine*. But it wasn't the complete story. You can still print that one. It's in your inbox right now."

Tara frowned at her computer screen and clicked around for a moment. She nodded curtly before looking back at Blake. It was now or never. Blake took a deep breath and handed a stack of papers to Tara, her heart and soul were on those pages and as they slipped from her hand, she knew there was no going back.

"But I also have this. I know I was supposed to stick to the review. But this story? It's *better* than a review. It's the entire reason Vella West exists as it is. And I think our readers will want to read something like this." Blake took a deep breath. "You asked for my best work. And, well, this was it."

Tara narrowed her eyes at Blake, but Blake didn't care. She was proud of that article, dammit. No matter what anyone said. Tara held up a finger, asking for a moment. Blake cleared her throat and said nothing.

Tara scanned the pages, her narrowed eyes giving away nothing. Blake hadn't expected her to read the entire thing right then, while Blake sat there silently watching and sort of wanting to disappear into the ether. Her entire heart was literally in her boss's hands.

When Tara finished reading she shuffled the papers, tapped them into a neat pile and stared at Blake.

"If it isn't the right fit, I understand. Maybe we can post it as a separate blog on social media? Or maybe we can—"

"Blake, are you quite finished?" Tara asked, her voice a bone-chilling monotone.

"Yes?" She hated that it came out like a question.

"Good." Tara dropped the papers on her desk and smirked. "Some free advice? Don't self-reject. You just handed me an amazing story and then cut it before I shared my thoughts."

Blake wanted to argue, but Tara was right.

That was exactly what she had done. “I understand.” Blake cleared her throat and sat up straighter. “Good advice.”

“I know,” Tara responded. She leaned back in her chair and crossed her arms. “It certainly isn’t on brand. And it needs some editing. Our readers might hate it. But I didn’t become editor in chief of this magazine without taking risks.”

Hope swelled inside Blake like a morning breeze rustling the poppies in the vineyard. Her story was worth the risk.

“Tara, I don’t know how to thank you.”

“Well,” Tara said with a frown. “Don’t thank me yet. But in for a penny, in for a pound. We’ve got to try something. And this might be just what we need. You’re sure she’ll sign off on this?”

“Who?” Blake assumed Tara would do the editing, but maybe she was wrong. She’d work with anyone Tara assigned. Her story, her and Sloane’s story, was going to be published.

“Sloane Vella. She’ll need to sign off on the story’s accuracy. She has to be okay with her story being in print. We’re going to need her to corroborate the details.”

Blake bit down on the edge of her lip. She hadn’t considered what this might mean for Sloane. For her vineyard. For Vella West.

“I’m sure,” Blake said. And she hoped she was right.

Sloane

Robby slid the stack of reviews across the desk, then nudged one final page toward her without a word.

Sloane's eyes caught the byline before she even saw the column heading: *Blake Escapes*. Her heart lurched, a familiar sense of dread sweeping over her as she glanced down. The travel magazine's logo loomed at the top of the page.

"You'll need to take a look at this one." They tapped the edge of the page. "It needs you to sign off on the facts."

Her fingers shook when she finally reached for the page, but she didn't pull it closer. It was Blake's story. Blake hadn't told her much about it and by the way Robby was looking at her now, she knew it couldn't be good. Had Blake given the resort a bad review?

Sloane let out a laugh, though it was more like a strangled sob. "If it's bad, just tell me now. I can handle it."

"Have you even talked to her?" Robby set down their stack of papers and leaned on the desk. "How have you not seen this?"

"A little." Sloane tucked a chunk of her black bob behind her ear and sighed. "I'm giving her space."

"Space? Nico leaves for Italy tomorrow. How much more time do you need?" Robby nudged the paper again, their voice louder this time. "Come on. Read it. Stop being so stubborn."

Sloane sat there for a moment, staring at the article, before Robby stormed out of the room. She was leaving for Europe tomorrow—everything was set. The hotel was in good shape, business booming. But something was wrong. She could feel it, that dark pull in her chest that had nothing to do with logistics, and everything to do with Blake. And whatever this was.

But she couldn't escape the pull. She shoved the paper aside for a while, distracted, but when the silence grew unbearable, she finally picked it up.

"Nowhere Else," by Blake Miller.

Her heart skipped a beat. That was it. The same Blake.

Sloane's hand shook as she touched the page. The years she had buried, the pain she'd tried to move past, rose to the surface like an unexpected wave.

She took a deep breath and began reading. Her eyes lingered on the opening lines:

> I never believed in forever—until I fell in love with her in Italy, ten years ago. We were young, reckless maybe, but what we

had was real. Deep and raw enough that even now, a decade later, it still aches to think about her. So, you can imagine my surprise when I walked into Vella West, fresh-faced and ready for my first job as a travel writer—and came face-to-face with my gorgeous, heartbreaking past.

Sloane couldn't breathe. The words hit her like a freight train, and she had to blink back tears.

But this isn't just a story about a chance reunion or lost time. It's about the silence that stretched between us, the years swallowed by mistakes and misunderstandings. It's about the quiet spaces filled with regret—and the faint, stubborn hope that maybe some things don't have to end. That love, no matter how tangled, can find its way back—like a secret whispered beneath the golden glow of a fading afternoon, hidden along winding vineyard trails, and carried softly on the breath of a dew-kissed morning.

She read it again. And again. By the third time, she was crying. And by the fourth, she was already halfway to her house.

This was terrible timing. She was leaving tomorrow. For Europe. With Nico.

"What happened to you?" Nico's voice cut through the haze of her thoughts as he dropped his duffel bag onto the rug.

Sloane sniffed, brushing the tears away. She waved absently at the papers. Nico picked them up and sat down at the table, reading the article quietly. The silence stretched between them, charged and full of unspoken words.

After a few minutes, Nico spoke, his voice soft but firm. "Sloane…you have to go to her."

Sloane blinked, almost startled by his directness. "What are you talking about? We leave tomorrow. I—"

Nico rolled his eyes, his tone growing impatient. "I can get myself to an internship, Sloane. You don't need to come."

Her breath caught. She swallowed hard. "I know you think that. But I can't just—"

Nico leaned forward, placing a hand on her shoulder, his voice gentle but resolute. "I know you, Sloane. I know you've put everything on hold—*everything*—for so long, and you've held this place together for years. But if you love her, you can't ignore what is *very clearly* a love letter back to you."

"It's not a love letter, it's an arti—"

"Sorry, cousin. You're wrong. This is top-tier love letter. You can ignore it, but is that really what you want? A chain of hotels, endlessly working? What do you want?"

Sloane wiped at her eyes and pulled her knees up to her chest. A decade of emotions that she'd stuffed down for so long came bubbling to the surface. "I don't know."

"I think you do. I think you want her. I think you want a chance to slow down. I think you should take it. This will all be here when you're ready. I'll be here. Robby will be here. Let us take care of you for once."

Sloane stared at him for a long moment. Nico wasn't a kid anymore. He wasn't the one who needed her to fix things anymore. The quiet realization hit her like a wave—maybe it was time to stop holding everything together for everyone else.

"I know you've always been there for me," Nico continued, his voice soft. "And I'll always need you—but not the way I used to. Let me go."

Sloane felt the weight of his words settle in her chest, a lump forming in her throat. She opened her mouth to protest, but Nico was already shaking his head.

"You've done everything for me, Sloane. You've done enough. Go to her. Please."

The weight of his words pushed Sloane further into the corner she'd been avoiding—the realization that if she didn't make a choice, she'd be stuck with the what-ifs forever. Nico wasn't a kid anymore, and Europe could wait. But the chance with Blake? That was something she couldn't put off.

Sloane took a deep breath, letting go of the final thread of hesitation. "What if she doesn't want me?" she asked, her voice barely above a whisper.

Nico's eyes softened. "But what if she does?"

Sloane nodded slowly, the fear still tight in her chest, but now, underneath it, there was something else. A spark of possibility.

"I have to go, don't I?"

Nico smiled, the same knowing grin from years ago. "Yeah, you do."

She laughed—a soft, shaky laugh—and grabbed her bag. "How did you get so smart about this love stuff?"

Nico rolled his eyes. "I am so not doing this with you," Nico laughed. "Now, go! I'll call you when I get there."

CHAPTER NINETEEN

Blake

THE CAR BARELY came to a stop before Blake stepped out in the early morning light, her flats landing softly on the warm stone of the circular drive. Summer had settled in like a heavy golden fog—thick with sunlight, soaked in heat that clung to her skin and made the world feel endless, as if the days would never slip away. Everything looked just as she remembered—maybe even sharper, more vivid. Or maybe it was just her, seeing the past through eyes that had been broken and rebuilt.

The antique doors loomed ahead, framed by ivy that had thickened and darkened under the relentless sun. The lavender was wild and rampant, spilling over the stone walls, heavy with scent—honeyed and sharp. Bees flitted between blossoms like they'd been invited to a secret party, carefree and buzzing with life. A butterfly drifted past her shoulder, fragile and unhurried, as if it knew she was coming home.

Blake adjusted the strap of her bag—a lighter load than last time. No laptop. No voice recorder. No backup outfit for wine tastings or fancy dinners. She hadn't even packed a swimsuit. This trip was different. It wasn't about work anymore. Not really.

Earlier that summer, she had come thinking this was just an assignment—a story to tell about a breathtaking, over-the-top resort that seemed too perfect to be real. Work. That was all. But she hadn't expected Sloane. Hadn't expected the flood of memories, the sharp ache of a laugh shared across a vineyard dinner table, or the ghost of a touch on a terrace railing. Their goodbye had never felt like an ending—more like a question mark hanging in the air, waiting for an answer.

Now, here she was. Not sent by an editor. Not chasing a deadline. Chasing a feeling. A hope. The part of her that still believed they weren't finished yet.

The heat wrapped around her, heavy with rosemary, lavender, and the bittersweet scent of memory.

Her fingers brushed the worn wood of the ancient doors. She swallowed hard and let a small, shaky smile slip free.

"Okay," she whispered to herself. "Let's try this again."

She stepped inside.

The lobby hadn't changed much—still the same soft light, the same polished floors—but there was a new floral arrangement on the large center table, lush and fragrant, like a silent promise of new beginnings. Behind the desk stood Robby, whose smile was warm but carried something else—something like a quiet sadness.

"Ms. Miller," Robby greeted, voice gentle but with a knowing edge. "I wasn't expecting to see you again so soon."

Blake forced her voice steady, even though her heart hammered in her chest. "Hello, Robby. Is Sloane here? I need to see her. I have to—"

Robby cut in with a teasing smirk. "I read your article."

Blake blinked, confused. "I'm sorry?"

"You didn't mention me once," Robby said, mock stern.

Her throat tightened. If Robby read the article, then maybe Sloane had seen it, too. "You read it? I told Tara I wanted to do this in person. Did… did she sign off on it?"

"Actually, I'm not sure. She took it with her. But I thought it was good. Except for forgetting to mention me—I'm kind of an important part of this place."

A small laugh escaped her lips. "I'll make sure to fix that next time."

Robby nodded. "Thank you. But Sloane's not here right now."

Her heart dropped. "No? But I thought she wasn't leaving until tomorrow."

Robby shrugged. "She hasn't been in the office since this morning. If I were you, I'd check the stables—she always says goodbye to the horses before she goes anywhere."

Blake pressed a quick kiss to Robby's cheek. They both blushed, but the warmth of the gesture steadied her nerves.

"Thank you, Robby. Really."

"I know."

Blake took off down the path, her hair streaming behind her in soft waves of caramel and gold. She was glad she wore flats instead of sandals—she needed to be quick. She wanted to call out Sloane's name until it echoed across the estate, wanted her to stop, turn around, come back. But when she rounded the corner, she saw it: a black car pulling away from the driveway.

"No, Sloane," she cried out, voice breaking like a fragile thread.

But the wind carried her words away. Sloane couldn't hear her. She hadn't called—hadn't reached out—and Blake hadn't even saved her number. The things Blake wanted to say couldn't be whispered over the phone. They needed to be said face-to-face, heart to heart.

Now Sloane was leaving for Europe without her.

Blake kept walking toward the house, not sure what she was searching for anymore. The ache inside her was a raw wound, open and bleeding.

Near the meadow, the two horses stood silently, watching. Blake stood beside them, tears spilling freely. She scratched at their noses, the familiar softness grounding her.

"I love her," she whispered, voice cracked. "I love her so much, and I don't want to say goodbye."

The words hung in the air, fragile and heavy.

And then, almost like a voice from within, a whisper answered: "So don't."

Blake's hands clenched into fists, nails digging into her palms. She closed her eyes and made a silent vow. She wouldn't let her go. Not like this. Not without a fight.

Because love wasn't about perfect timing or neat endings. It was messy. It was hard. It was painful. But it was real.

And if she had to chase Sloane halfway across the world, if she had to break down every wall and tear down every doubt—she would.

Because some things were worth every risk.

Sloane

Sloane had never been good at goodbyes. In fact, she had been a master at avoiding them. Her life, the mess of it all, had been full of those—so many little departures that had added up to one giant, painful absence. She had thought it was easier this way, walking away before someone else could.

Nico was going to be fine. He was studying abroad for the summer, not leaving forever. He would love Italy, just as she had. And he'd come home with a stronger sense of what running a vineyard might be like. If that was what he wanted.

If not, that would be okay, too. Blake wasn't going to force her dreams on Nico. She loved running this place. She especially loved the thrill of restoring and getting it up and running. Robby was the one who was good at keeping it going. Blake would love to see it. She could still hear Blake's voice in her head, so clear it might have been a whisper in the room with her.

Sloane turned away from the window. She'd packed all the things she thought she'd need, but none of it felt right. She didn't need a passport or a suitcase full of memories that no longer fit. She needed one thing.

Blake.

The thought crashed into her like a wave, sweeping away all the plans she'd made for herself, for Nico, for the future that she had thought would be hers. What was she doing? She couldn't leave. Not with everything left unsaid again.

Sloane grabbed her bag and tossed it into the corner, pulling on her shoes with shaky hands. She didn't care about running anymore. All she could think about was finding Blake. She'd go to San Diego. She'd find her on her next writing assignment. Whatever it took.

When she reached the stables, she noticed someone talking to her horses. No, not *someone*, Blake. There she was, standing tall in the morning light, her face bathed in a glow that almost made Sloane believe this was a dream. A second chance.

Blake's eyes met hers and the world seemed to stop. The horses shifted restlessly behind them, but for Sloane, there was only Blake—everything else faded away.

"I was scared," Sloane whispered, her voice trembling. She didn't care anymore if Blake understood. She needed to say it all. "I ghosted you not because I didn't care, but because I was terrified. Terrified you'd see my family's mess. Terrified you'd think you had to help me raise a kid when we were still just kids ourselves."

Blake's gaze softened, and Sloane's walls—built so high, so carefully—cracked, and everything she had tried to bury came rushing forward.

"I read your article. Blake, it was beautiful," Sloane said, her voice breaking. "I'll sign off on it. I'll sign anything you need."

Blake let out a soft laugh. "Thanks. I don't know what's next, but I do know this—I'm done letting other people write my story."

Sloane took a step closer, her heart pounding. "What about me?"

Blake's hand reached for hers, soft but steady. "What about you?"

"Is there room in your future for someone like me? Someone stubborn and still full of grief?" Sloane asked, almost afraid to hear the answer.

Blake's fingers traced light patterns up Sloane's arms. "Someone kind? Fiercely loyal. Someone who'd give everything for her family."

Sloane swallowed hard. "Blake, if you keep touching me like that, I'm going to kiss you."

Blake leaned in, voice low and daring. "If you kiss me, I might tell you I love you, Sloane Vella."

Sloane closed her eyes, breath catching. "Good, because I love you, Blake. I think I've loved you this whole time. I just didn't know how to carry it all, so I hid it away." The world had narrowed to just the two of them—the thundering beat of her heart, Blake's hand on her skin, the pull between them undeniable. For a moment, everything else disappeared.

"I love you, too." Blake said. "We'll figure it all out. Together."

But then Sloane pulled back just enough to whisper, her voice full of trembling hope, "I'm not leaving for Europe, Blake. I stayed because I had to find you."

Blake's eyes widened. "You…you stayed?"

"I was going to go with him because I was afraid to let him to do it alone. I was afraid to admit that he didn't need me anymore," Sloane admitted, "but my heart has always been here. With you. I was scared, Blake. But I'm not running anymore. I want to be with you."

Blake

Blake's breath hitched. The raw emotion in Sloane's voice made her chest tighten. Slowly, Blake cupped her face, eyes brimming with tears, and leaned in for a kiss. It wasn't just any kiss—it was everything. It was the apology, the promise, the hope for what could still be.

"I love you," Blake whispered, her words barely a breath.

Sloane's lips curled into a smile as she kissed Blake again, deeper, letting everything else fall away.

"I love you, too."

They stood there, wrapped in each other, letting the kiss say everything the words couldn't. The world outside—the perfect world of the resort, the carefully planned events, the polished image—faded to nothing. There was only this: the quiet, the warmth, the certainty that they were finally, finally here.

Sloane's arms curled around Blake as if she would never let go, her fingers pressing into Blake's skin like a silent promise. Blake's chest tightened with an overwhelming tenderness, and for the first time in what felt like forever, she didn't feel *lost*. She felt home.

When they finally pulled apart, breathless and wide-eyed, the moment stretched out around them. It wasn't *just* about the kiss. It was about the understanding, the unspoken bond that neither of them had realized was so desperately needed until now.

Blake cupped Sloane's cheek, her thumb brushing over the softness of her skin. "I'm not going anywhere," she said quietly. "Not this time."

Sloane smiled, a small, fragile thing, as she nodded. "Good."

They didn't need more words. Not yet. Not now.

There was only the gentle, slow pull into the cottage. Into each other. And the quiet, inevitable way they moved together, no longer held back by fear, by time, or by the walls they'd built around themselves.

EPILOGUE

Blake

THE EVENING SUN sank beyond the last hill as Blake and Sloane watched from a blanket in the grass. Winnie and Rhett drank from the stream nearby as crickets began their evening chirp in the mid-July sunset.

"Alright, Miller. I'm done with work for the day. You've dragged me all the way out here. I know you have something to tell me. Spill it." Sloane dug her fingertips into the soft flesh at Blake's hip, making her giggle.

"The numbers are in." Blake held her breath. They'd been waiting on the magazine's sale numbers. The numbers that held Blake's writing career in her hands.

"And?"

Blake blew out a breath. "Consistent overall. Tara said that the initial spike in sales due to the originality of my article helped counterbalance the…dip in sales after the first few days."

"So, what does that mean?" Sloane leaned forward and pressed a kiss to Blake's temple. She tucked the hair behind her ear and kept nuzzling, kissing.

"I can't think when you're doing that," Blake chided. Sloane nuzzled in closer before her soft laughter tickled Blake's neck and she relented. "It means no more articles like this one. Tara said if I want to write for *Elsewhere*, I'll need to change my tactic."

"Blake, I'm so sorry," Sloane said. And Blake knew she meant it, too. They'd had some time to talk about their future. Blake wanted to keep writing. But she knew now, she didn't want to write bite-sized social media posts and travel articles.

"I think I'm okay with it," she said, sighing. "The good news is, there was a big uptick on social media followings. For some reason, the algorithm loved me. Loved *us*. They especially liked your wildflower fields."

Sloane bit her lip. "You know I'm going to have to ask Robby what all this means later right?"

"It means… I quit." Blake felt a giant weight lift when she said the words. "I think I'm going to take my journals, my notebooks, and see about turning them into a blog. I want to be my own boss and write about…whatever I do next. Whether it's traveling, or…"

"Or?"

"Well, you know how you've been wanting to give Robby more responsibility?" Sloane nodded and Blake felt hope bloom in her chest. It was now or never. Last time they had a plan, Sloane had bolted. But it was different now. She hoped.

"I was thinking that maybe, if you did—if you turned over the resort to them, just for a little while…maybe we could finally do the Italy trip. Again."

"You want to go back with me?" Sloane's eyes looked wet with tears.

"I want to go everywhere with you, Sloane Vella." Blake leaned forward and pressed a soft kiss to Sloane's mouth. "Will you go back with me?"

"Yes," Sloane whispered when she finally broke their kiss. "It will take some time. I need to get everything organized, and train Robby on some of the protocols. But, yes. I'll go anywhere with you."

Six months later

The road twisted, narrow and uneven, winding through the verdant hills as Sloane's hands gripped the wheel, her jaw set in that quiet determination that always made Blake's heart flutter. She didn't know where they were headed, but Blake did—every curve of this road, every shift in the landscape felt like a pull from the past, a thread she was about to tug.

Blake had never imagined it would be like this. That she would return to this place—the one they'd found together so many years ago when everything felt possible and no dream was too big. The farmhouse was still here, still waiting for them.

"Just up ahead," Blake said, her voice thick with emotion. She looked out the window, trying to ignore the flutter of nerves in her stomach. She had to get this right.

They were nearly there. The vineyard was spread out before them, the vines twisted and aged, but still strong. The house, nestled among them, stood just as it had all those years ago: tired but full of potential, like a forgotten dream ready to be revived.

As the car rounded the final bend, the farmhouse appeared in full view, surrounded by fields of grapevines that were wild and overgrown. The stone walls were cracked in places, but they held a quiet kind of strength. The windows, dusty and boarded up, had an air of mystery—like secrets were waiting to be discovered.

Sloane didn't say anything at first, her gaze

caught by the sight of the place, but Blake could see the recognition in her eyes, the flicker of memory that passed over her features.

"I remember," Sloane murmured, her voice hushed, almost reverent. Her hands relaxed on the wheel, and Blake watched as her lips parted in disbelief. "We used to talk about it. About fixing it up. Living here."

Sloane shook her head, a laugh slipping past her lips, tinged with wonder. "I didn't think it could ever be real."

Blake's heart swelled; her chest tight with the weight of everything that had come before this moment. The years apart, the distance they'd created between them—this house was the one thing that had always remained, a promise unfulfilled, a dream they'd shared on a blanket under the stars.

"I didn't either," Blake said softly, her gaze steady on Sloane. She reached over, her fingers brushing against Sloane's, an unspoken reassurance. "But it's for sale now. And it's ours if we want it."

Sloane's eyes widened, a flicker of something deep—hope, maybe, or fear—crossing her features. She turned to Blake, her expression unreadable, but Blake knew. She knew the weight of that question. This was it, the choice to step forward, to take the leap.

"I want it," Sloane said, her voice low but steady. "I want it with you."

Blake smiled, the kind of smile that was full of promises. "Good. I was hoping you would say that."

She opened the door and stepped out into the warm Tuscan air, the scent of earth and vines mixing with the distant sea breeze. The sun was beginning to dip low in the sky, casting long shadows across the property. There was so much to fix, so much to rebuild, but there was something about the place—about the history of it—that felt right.

Sloane followed her, her boots crunching on the gravel path as they moved toward the house. They walked through the overgrown garden, now untamed but still filled with beauty—wildflowers peeking out from the weeds, vines climbing over forgotten trellises. The house loomed ahead of them, the stone steps cracked but sturdy, the wood of the shutters weathered and worn.

Blake reached out, tracing her fingers over the wall, her touch lingering as though the house itself was alive, holding memories of the past. This was where their future could begin.

"We'll fix it," Blake said, her voice soft, almost reverent. "We'll make it ours."

Sloane turned to her, eyes full of affection

and something deeper—something she didn't need to say, because Blake already understood. They would do this together. Just like they'd always dreamed.

Sloane

The warmth of the stone under her palm grounded her as she took in the familiar sight of the farmhouse. The same house that had been a dream so many years ago. Back then, it had felt like a wild, impossible idea—an abandoned place that existed only in their shared fantasy, a dream whispered between them under the blanket of stars.

But now, here it was. And it was real.

Sloane's pulse thrummed in her ears as she looked at Blake. She could still see the girl she'd fallen in love with—unpredictable, wild, full of hope and promise. She saw it in the way Blake's eyes shone when she spoke about this place, the quiet confidence that radiated from her as she laid out the future they could build.

They'd talked about this when they were younger—before life had swept them in different directions, before they'd been torn apart by circumstances they hadn't yet learned to navigate. But this farmhouse, this life, had always been there, waiting for them to come back. Waiting for them to choose it. Choose each other.

And Sloane was ready. More than ready. She had been dreaming of this moment her entire life—of settling into a life that felt like home. But now, standing here with Blake, the weight of it all settled on her chest.

It wasn't just the farmhouse, the vineyard, the life in Italy. It was *this*. It was the way Blake made her feel alive in a way no one else ever had. It was the way Blake made the impossible seem like the most natural thing in the world.

Sloane turned to her, her heart in her throat. "I've spent my whole life running," she said, her voice thick with emotion. "But this…this is what I've always wanted. With you. This. *Us*."

Blake reached out, cupping her face, her thumb brushing gently over her skin. "I've always known that Sloane," she whispered, her voice low, full of meaning. "This isn't just a house. This is home."

Sloane leaned into the touch, her heart pounding as she looked up at Blake. The sky above them had turned a deep violet, the first stars twinkling in the evening sky. It felt like a sign, like the universe was aligning.

But there was one more thing she needed to say. One more thing she needed to ask.

"Sloane," Blake murmured, stepping closer.

But Sloane wasn't waiting anymore. She took a step back, dropped to one knee in the soft grass, and held out the ring that had been waiting for this moment. The sapphire gleamed in the fading light, a symbol of all they had been through and all they still had to look forward to. She could feel the weight of it in her hand—the weight of the years, the heartache, the hope.

"Blake," she said, her voice steady but full of love. "I'm ready for one more adventure with you. The kind that lasts forever. Will you marry me?"

Blake's eyes filled with surprise, then joy, as she knelt in front of Sloane, taking the ring and slipping it onto her finger. "Yes," she whispered, her voice breaking.

Sloane closed the distance between them, pressing her lips to Blake's in a kiss that sealed everything—the past, the present, the future. This was home. This was everything they'd ever wanted. And it was just the beginning.

* * * * *